SCRAGGLE

ERIC

MATTHEW

GORLOW

Noyrog
Publishing

The following is an account of the events
as they happened,
nothing more and nothing less.

Contents

Chapter 1
DUST

Santa Fe, New Mexico. Early morning. The sun has yet to show its face, but the earth is already warming and creatures stirring in anticipation of the day. Piñon trees, yucca, and the occasional cacti spread across the dusty landscape. Adobe homes, each a slightly different shade of brown from the next and so natural to their surroundings that they might easily be mistaken for part of the terrain, scatter through the hills and along the arroyo as it twists through the land.

One particular home, teetering right near the edge of the arroyo, has a back yard that leads off into a small Native American graveyard. Walking through the middle of this graveyard is…Dustin. The few — or rather, the single person — who knows him as more than just an acquaintance — refers to him as "Dusty," a thin twelve-year-old boy, with disheveled, dusty brown hair, currently robed in an oversized hand-me-down sweater and well-worn jeans, carrying a beat up old turquoise backpack, as muscle memory navigates him through the ins and outs of the graveyard.

The graves themselves are marked only by nondescript piles of rock and dead flowers. On occasion, a mourner, remembering the loved one they once knew, comes to rebuild the piled rocks and replenish the dying flowers with fresh ones, until one year they can no longer make it, and the flowers turn to dust, and the rocks become part of the landscape, and time forgets that someone was ever buried there.

Dusty exits the graveyard onto a lonely dirt road. In the 1920s, this road was bustling with cars and carriages kicking up clouds of dust as they bounced along into town, but since then, elaborate paved highways have been built and the town's population has stretched off in a different direction. Like the graves, time will one day forget the little dirt road, but for the time being, Dusty is glad he gets to walk on it every day, just him and the abandoned road…. Well, lately, there has been another *presence*.

Dusty walks in the center of the road, sliding his feet through the dirt and kicking up rocks.

Suddenly he stops, self-aware.

He looks back.

There, standing not twenty feet away from him, is the other *presence*, a coyote.

It sits back on its hind legs, staring at him.

Dusty returns the gaze, studying the creature's features, its keen ears and snout, its vivid eyes and powerfully unaffected expression.

Dusty can hear the sounds of the morning around them, the dirt and rocks shifting as the morning light continues to grow warmer. The scent of dry piñon begins to bake into the morning air. For some reason, this precursor to the heated day reminds him of where he is supposed to be. Dusty turns back and keeps walking.

He can't remember the first time he saw the coyote. Sometimes it feels like it's always been there, but he knows that's not true. He's only lived here a few months now. If he had to guess, the coyote maybe showed up after the first month; he remembers it was cold when he first saw it, bitter cold.

Dusty cuts off the road and into the denser terrain; piñons, cacti, and chamisa shrubs scatter along the line of the arroyo. This section of the arroyo is thin; down by his house it is wide, varying between twenty to one hundred feet across and at least fifty feet at the deepest point. Here, it is only five or six feet deep and three or four feet across. He walks along the top of it, occasionally hopping over to the other side.

Ducking under an intertwined group of piñons, he comes to a chain link fence. On the other side of the fence is a school: three trailer buildings, a jungle gym, some beat-up basketball courts, a field, and a large adobe building in the distance. Beneath the fence, a well-worn path is dug into the dirt. Dusty climbs under, but his backpack gets stuck on the fence, ripping open as he comes up on the other side. His books and colored pencils scatter in the dirt. He picks them up, one by one. Perhaps he has even left some of them unfound, but he does not seem to mind. Stuffing one last handful of dust and pencils into the bag, he tries to re-zip it, but the zipper is now torn off the tracks.

The school bell rings.

He grips the broken flap closed and shuffles onward, holding the backpack together with both hands in front of him.

Meanwhile, inside one of the trailer buildings, Miss Gutierrez is calling attendance. Born in South Africa to Mexican parents and educated in England, she considers herself to be quite an authority on the ways of the world. Thirty-four years young, with long black curly hair, a youthful face and voice (which she struggles to counter with an assertive tone), she goes down the list.

"Gabe?

"Uh…here."

"Nicole?"

"Present."

"Hector?"

Hector raises his hand.

Not hearing a response, she looks up.

"Please respond verbally when I call your name. It simply makes it go a lot faster if I don't have to look around, look up, look down. It's…and furthermore, it's polite, as you know, when someone is addressing you verbally, to acknowledge them back verbally! It's polite…to communicate. Communication is key! It is the very base, the very glue of society. Without it…"

Hector relents. "Present."

Miss Gutierrez is satisfied. She goes back to roll call, clearing her throat. "Dusti…?"

She remembers noticing that he was not in his chair as the bell rang. And if he's not in his chair, then he's not in the classroom, because she's certainly never seen him hanging around socializing with any of the other students. So she raises her pencil to mark him absent. Just before her pencil can make its mark…

"Here."

Dusty's voice.

But he's not here. She looks up, confused. The students look confused, too. Just then, Dusty walks in, still gripping his dirt-covered backpack in front of him. All eyes shift over to him. He beelines to his desk, a few colored pencils spilling out along the way. Chuckles murmur through the room.

Miss Gutierrez snaps out of it, no longer enchanted by Dusty's strange timing and the paper thinness of their trailer-classroom walls… "That's a tardy, Dustin."

But Dusty does not look up. He gets out a pencil and a notepad from his backpack and places them on his desk and starts drawing. Baffled, Miss Gutierrez moves on. "Megan?"

"Present."

Meanwhile, Dusty picks the wood away from the lead tip of his pencil. He can't remember if he has a pencil sharpener somewhere in the bottom of his backpack, but it doesn't matter. He enjoys doing it this way. He finally gets enough visible lead to write, but this time he lifts up the notepad from his desk, using it as a secrecy-shield for what's underneath. There on the desk is an intricate penciled drawing of his daily visitor, the coyote. He continues, adding to the deeply etched and detailed lines of this sketch.

—

Recess. The other students play in the sun: some play basketball, some play football; groups of girls walk around, giggling, snacking on candy.

There is only one tree in the schoolyard, and hence, only one area of shade: an old fifty-foot cottonwood and underneath it, an old set of forgotten, rusty monkey bars. Dusty is alone. The other kids are too grown up for monkey bars; after all, they're in the sixth grade, almost teenagers now. Dusty climbs to the top and walks across them; he dangles upside down until he nearly loses consciousness, slowly sliding off and landing like a pile of sludge on the ground. When the glimmers of sharp white fade from his vision and he has gathered his balance, he turns to the enduring cottonwood.

He climbs the tree, as high as he can, until he reaches a limb that will surely snap if he goes any further…and then, he climbs back to the middle and sits on a sturdy limb looking out over the sun-washed schoolyard.

He watches: some kids run around, playing together; some argue with each other — others pretend to ignore one another. Dusty leans back on the trunk. He crosses his arms and stretches his legs out on the branch. A sudden gust of wind would surely send him hurtling to the hard ground below, but he doesn't seem to notice. He closes his eyes.

The school bell rings.

He climbs down from his cottonwood, getting sap on his hand as he does; he wipes most of it on the front of his pants. But his hand is still sticky, so he forcefully rubs his palms together. The friction creates tiny rolls of sap and dirt that he inspects closely, before knocking them off one at a time.

The other students are shuffling back toward the classroom. Dusty heads to the end of the line, still rubbing his hands together to create new rolls of dirt. Gabe and Anthony come running in behind him.

As they start to push ahead of him, Gabe notices the dark sap smudge on the front of Dusty's pants and stops. "You piss on yourself?"

Gabe taps Anthony and points his attention toward the spot on Dusty's pants. "He peed himself."

Anthony chimes in: "That's gross, what'd you do, man?"

Gabe snickers. "He pissed himself."

Anthony gives a half chuckle, but quickly loses interest. Gabe is not satisfied. He tries to rally Megan on the other side of him. "Look! Dustin pissed his pants."

"Ewwww. Gross!"

Finally getting the response he wanted, Gabe soaks it up with laughter. Dusty keeps shuffling ahead, leaving them behind as they continue to bond over their disgust.

The students file into the classroom. Dusty heads straight for his desk and takes out his pencil and shielding notepad. The other students converse and dally about, as they settle into their desks. Miss Gutierrez cuts through the clatter with her crisp voice. "What's the definition of a challenge?"

She dives into her vehemence. Dusty ducks into his coyote sketch.

"What challenges us is what defines us."

He occasionally looks up, watching the enthralling intensity and strong sense of belief in her expressions and gestures. "…the importance of having a plan to work through such challenges…"

Her energy seems boundless; and well into the afternoon, her conducting gestures have lost none of their conviction. She is working herself into a lather, as if she is trying to reach some kind of catharsis through her explanations.

Eventually, the bell rings, popping the air out of the ballooning frenzy. But before she lets them go, she passes around a sheet of paper for homework. There are three questions on it, each to be answered in a paragraph below:

1. What is a challenge you face in your everyday life?

2. How do you think you can overcome this challenge?

3. Discuss a challenge you have overcome in the past.

———

Dusty walks back through the Native American graveyard, the crunch of dirt and dry twigs beneath his feet, but he is not headed for his home. Instead, he veers off to the right, arriving at the edge of the deepest part of the arroyo.

He makes his way toward a little cave carved into the arroyo's brim, a secret spot, with a large shrub growing down over its entrance, disguising it from all except the fated wanderer who might stumble upon its existence.

From this spot, Dusty can look below — fifty feet down — into the nearly dry river bottom, but he doesn't look down; he has seen it many times. Instead, he leans back against the cool dirt wall of his hideout and looks out over at the scattered houses above the arroyo. The shrub that grows over his little cave keeps him hidden from the rest of the world, but is perforated enough for him to peer outward.

Off to the left, he can see his house and his sister through the living room window. Her brow furrowed, she sits…and stands…and sits…and stands.

Suddenly, off to his right, something pops into view, then back down out of sight. What was that? He wasn't sure how close it was. It happened so fast. Again. But this time he can see. It's a human face. Across the arroyo. There. And back down again. Up again. Now a different face. Kids, flying up and back down in the yard across the arroyo.

He sneaks down the canyon and up the other side. Quietly maneuvering up against an old wood and wire fence on the edge of the curious yard, Dusty spies through the dry weeds growing up over it.

He sees three kids jumping on a trampoline — two girls and one boy. One of the girls appears to be four or five years younger than Dusty; the boy is probably a couple years older than he is, and the other girl is the same age as him. In fact, he's seen her before, at school — not in his class, but in the other sixth grade class in the trailer next door.

Though he is aware that the other two kids are there, he simply cannot take his eyes off the girl his age. She lets her legs give out and lazily lies on the trampoline as the other kids jump around her. She grabs at their legs and they screech and laugh, narrowly escaping her grasp.

"Dusty...!» His sister's voice calls out over the arroyo.

Dusty comes back to himself. The kids on the trampoline look out across the arroyo. Realizing he had begun to stand up to look at the trampoline girl, Dusty ducks.

"Dusty...!"

Dusty begins to sneak back down into the arroyo. He can hear giggling from the trampoline behind him and the boy's voice, mocking the call.

"Dusty!?"

Dusty scampers through the arroyo, cutting along the sandy river bed toward his house. And just before he is about to turn and go up the other side, he notices a strange amber glow coming from where the arroyo bottom wiggles into a tunnel up ahead.

He rarely comes this way; but even so, he has seen that tunnel a few times before and it never had this strange amber glow. The light is oddly consuming without being bright, flowing outward, permeating, painting the air.

"Dusty!"

Drawing his attention back, he makes haste up the arroyo and hurries around the house to the front.

A few yards out from the front gate stands his sister. She is rubbing the fabric together on the bottom of her sweater, like a child does to their blanket. The fabric has become worn in this spot through years of gentle abuse. This hypnotic comfort or slow torture of fabric (depending on whose side you're on) has been dubbed "nicing" by his sister. She's not sure why, but the name does seem to fit the action. In fact, at one point she decided that if the *why* were explored deeply enough, it would take away from the true and cosmic fit of a thing simply being what it is. So, to her, this is "nicing." She enjoys this a lot: finding names for things that have not yet been defined, or in her opinion have been named in an unsuitable manner.

His sister greets him with hugs. "Where've you been?"

He starts to answer, but doesn't really know what to say. As much as he could tell, he was just off being himself, but he doesn't know how to say that without making it sound rude. So instead, a strange, but friendly noise makes its way out of his mouth. A mixture of "um…" and "hi." She is used to these responses from him. She doesn't know why he says so little, or why he mumbles when he does, but it is familiar to her and brings her comfort. To her, it's just in his nature.

As they walk inside, she asks him if they kept him after school.

He shakes his head no.

She gives him another squeeze and shuts the door.

Chapter 2
MIST - THE SPIDER HAND

A beat-up old boom box is tuned in to the oldies station on the kitchen counter. Dusty's sister cooks homemade egg rolls, a recipe their mom had learned from a neighbor in San Francisco — a place and time his sister talks about often. Dusty was too young to remember much of it. He remembers his bright yellow slippers with puffy rubber bird heads sticking up on the toes that would bounce as he walked. He wore them everywhere he went. And he remembers brown — lots of brown: brown wood chips on the playground floor and brown rubber covering the jungle gym, brown carpet, and faux-wood wallpaper.

His sister tries to talk over the radio. "This is the one thing your mother used to cook better than me."

She has always referred to their mother as his. He doesn't know why she does this, but he's always respected whatever reasons she has for disassociating herself with their parents, so he's never protested or pried, though at times he wonders if she wishes he would.

Dusty sits on the large adobe banco, a window sill doubling as a bench in the living room. He has the homework from class in front of him, but he is not answering the questions. In place of a written paragraph, he has started another sketch of the coyote, but at the moment, he is not drawing. He is staring out the window, across the arroyo, at the house with the trampoline. He can barely see into the yard. A large piñon blocks his view of where the actual trampoline and "the trampoline girl" would be.

His sister raises her voice, competing with the radio again. "If it's no good, we don't eat, ok? We just order pizza..."

He keeps staring at the trampoline house. The warm brown light of the sun is dissolving, and a new pale glow is replacing it. Dusty looks up to see the moon. A small part of it peeks out from behind a thick gray cloud, luminous, yet pallid.

It starts to drizzle.

Dusty draws his gaze back to earth. The raindrops pitter-patter on the large limestones in the back yard. Suddenly, he notices a large dusty handprint on one of the stones — *at least three times the length of a large human hand!*

The drizzle turns to rain.

His sister calls again from the kitchen. "It's ready…"

His focus remains on the handprint; *besides its uncanny size, it also has only four digits, which consist of three long thin fingers, and an equally long thumb, sprouting off to the side.*

His sister is getting anxious. "Come and get it…"

Dusty turns to her, but then turns right back to the window. The print is nearly gone. He watches closely, as the rain washes the rest of it away.

"What do you want to drink? We've got ginger ale — if you want."

Dusty comes and sits at the dining table as his sister brings them each an oversized egg roll and places a big bowl full of them in the center of the table. She sits and begins to eat, but Dusty does not. His attention is still out the window.

"Is it ok?" She asks.

Without looking at his plate, he takes a bite; his mind stays outside. She is a good cook and she knows it. She started collecting *Bon Appetite* magazines at the age of seven and by twelve she was cooking intricate Thanksgiving feasts for the family. Usually, her food is the one thing she can tell he is excited about.

She pushes the subject further. "It's not very good, is it?"

He takes another bite. "It's good. I like it."

She doesn't buy it. "You don't have to eat it."

He raises the egg roll up to his mouth, but his concentration drifts back outside and the egg roll lowers back down again. This happens several times before she cannot take it anymore. "Stop. Don't eat that."

She stands up and takes the egg roll out of his hands and starts clearing the plates from the table. "Don't waste your hunger on that, it's gross…it's no good. We'll order our pizza. You don't have to…I'm sorry. It's gross, don't worry. It's quick, though; it gets here ten minutes before they say it will…. Usually."

She rushes over to the kitchen, dumping the serving bowl full of egg rolls into the trash.

Dusty doesn't know what happened, but he can tell she is upset. He gets up and walks into the kitchen, quietly standing next to her. Out the kitchen window he can see the rain has slowed again to a drizzle and the night is closing in.

She reaches over for the cordless phone and dials the number off a fridge magnet. Finally, exhaling, she turns to him and kisses his head. As she does, out of the corner of his eye Dusty notices a large shadow move past the kitchen window, blocking the porch light for a brief second! *What was that!?*

Then, the voice on the other end of the phone: "June Love Pizza, how can I help you?"

His sister picks at the uneaten food she cleared from the table, popping scraps in her mouth in between sentences. "Hi, we'd like a delivery, please."

Dusty pulls himself up on the counter with his hands to look out the window, to see what caused the shadow...nothing there...just desert shrubs, the familiar piñon trees, and dirt turning to mud, all lit by the eerie, powerful moonlight.

His sister continues on the phone.
Following the direction in which the shadow had headed, Dusty moves toward the living room window. He cautiously peers out: everything is still, wet, and glistening. He can now see the moon clearly. Full, beaming like a beacon, it has never seemed so close, so tangible, as if he could reach it if he kept running toward it. He looks back down to earth.... Nothing.... Nothing moving, at least...except for a few

earthworms poking out of the fresh mud, and certainly nothing that could have caused the shadow.

"Pizza is on the way!"

———

By and by, they munch on pizza as his sister rubs the worn-out spot on her sweater, "nicing" it like a blankie.

When they've had their fill, they tidy up and head off to bed.

———

In his room, Dusty settles into the covers, feeling the cool sheets as his legs search for a comfortable spot. The moonlight floods in through the window by his bed. Only his eyes and nose stick up out of the covers; his legs slowly keep moving, searching for warmth.

There is the soft sound of drizzling rain on his window pane.

His legs stop and he starts to drift off. His eyes close. He sleeps....

He sits on the ground with his back against a wall. He cannot tell where he is. There is only darkness. He can barely see his own hands in front of him. Suddenly, he feels something touch his ankle, a gentle squeeze — a hand. He hears a whisper, a girl's voice.

"Is that you?"

The hand moves to his shoulder; the girl slowly crawls closer. He wants to say yes, but he doesn't know if she means him when she says "you." His silence does not stop her. She cuddles up next to him. He can feel the shape of her ear and the texture of her hair as her head presses against his neck — the trampoline girl.

Suddenly, a new presence emerges, darker than the shadows. Lurking. Closer. Closer. The trampoline girl begins to squeeze him tighter. The presence looms directly over them. Consuming. Dusty tries to move them away from it. But, he is frozen inside his own body. He thrashes inwardly, fighting his paralysis.

…Dusty's eyes flutter open.

A dark shadow looms over him. He fights for his consciousness, trying to fully awaken. The shadow moves away. Finally, fully awake, his eyes dart to the window, catching a glimpse of – *A DARK HAND* on the outer window sill. A split second — then it's gone. Dusty stays frozen, eyes fixed out the window. *What was it he saw?* It looked like huge, long, leathery spider legs, but he knows they were fingers. He remembers the ominous handprint he saw earlier.

He slowly slips out of bed. Staying low, he slinks up to the wall under the window and inches up, little by little, until he can peer out. The wet trees glisten like sharp metal in the moonlight. He is too short to see any lower. *What is on the other side of the wall, beneath the window outside?* That is where the owner of the hand must have been, or maybe, still is….

He grabs the nightstand and props it under the window to get a better view. He steps on top and rises up…slowly…. There, in the wet dirt, an imprint — *like a rabbit's footprint, but much, much bigger — like a kangaroo, maybe?* Behind it is another — and another. The odd footprints start at the edge of the arroyo and lead right up to his window. He thinks of the shadow hovering over him. *Adrenaline.* He gets down and heads for his bedroom door. He stiffly turns the handle; the door creaks open.

He pokes his head into the dark hallway. He listens…it is quiet. He can see light from the moon beaming into the hall from the large window in the foyer. He tiptoes forward.

Coming into the foyer, he keeps his eyes locked on the window by the front door. As bright and luminous as the moon is, the shadows and crevices of the night are equally cosmic in their darkness and density, providing a welcome hiding place for the unknown. Never taking his attention away from the window, Dusty makes his way around and up the stairs toward his sister's room, turning his head only once the window is out of view.

The door to his sister's bedroom is slightly open. He peeks in. She is asleep on the bed. Her face is turned down and away, her feet tangled in the covers. He tiptoes around the bed to the side table. Now, he can see his sister's face. She looks worn out, her brow crumpled and worried, amidst an anxious dream. She is the only person he has ever been close to, but in this moment, she looks so unfamiliar and far away.

He opens the bedside table drawer and fishes through the pill containers until he finds a flashlight, then slinks back out the door.

He heads down the stairs into the foyer.

He points the flashlight at the window.... Nothing but the reflection of the light. He walks closer to get a better view outside. He moves the flashlight around, breaking up the darkness and shadow. He sees what's always there: the limestone pavement, cacti, and piñon trees.... A jackrabbit scuffles forward a bit and resettles deeper under a yucca plant.

He turns off the flashlight and remains still for a while.

He swallows, jump-starting the breath back into his body.

He opens the foyer closet and puts on his shoes and jacket. His pulse moves down to his stomach. His heartbeat is slow, but each beat shakes his entire body. He swings open the door, turning the flashlight back on.

He goes outside.

The drizzle has shrunk into minute droplets, softly blowing back and forth in the night air…but he cannot hear any wind.

It's quiet.

He tries to match the silence, but his footsteps on the grit-covered limestone won't let him. No matter how softly he tries to tread, each step belligerently eats away at the delicate silence. He knows the limestone path ends at the front gate. He rushes forward, to get it over with.

At the gate, he unlatches it and pushes it outward. As it drifts open, the hinges let out a doleful whine. He scans with the flashlight — *nothing*. He steps down into the mud; it hugs the soles of his shoes, feebly begging him to stay with each step, as he moves to the side of the house.

Around the next corner is the outside of his bedroom window. He peeks his head around — *nothing there*. He shines the flashlight into the dark brush on the other side of the window, dissecting the shadows — and before he knows it, he has carried himself forward and is under his window. He kneels down and examines the print. It looks like a large paw with a bone-like indentation behind it. The entire print has to be nearly two thirds the length of his own leg. He searches for another print. Indeed, the tracks appear to have come from — as well as to lead off toward — the arroyo. His legs take over. Alert, but timid, they carefully carry him, following the tracks toward the arroyo.

As he moves away from the house, larger looming trees cultivate deeper shadows, but he keeps his flashlight focused on the tracks. The prints seem to be oddly spaced: two steps close together, followed by a gap, but in the middle of each gap there are two new prints. He looks closer at these — they are wider apart from one another than the other steps, and are a sort of rectangle made of three long, bony ridges, perhaps a fist from the skeletal hand.

Dusty stops at the edge of the arroyo, pointing the flashlight down into its depths. He cannot tell where the tracks lead from here; the downward grade of the arroyo is too steep to leave distinguishable marks. The night's rain has left a thin stream of water, now slicing through the arroyo bottom, fervently dodging between brittle rock and mud to find the lowest point. Off to the far left, the faint amber glow that he saw earlier today still seeps from where the arroyo turns into a tunnel.

The mist begins to turn back to drizzle.

He looks back up at the moon.

He heads back to the house.

Once inside, he shuts the front door behind him, puts the flashlight on the window sill, and takes off his jacket. He hangs it in the foyer closet and sits on the floor to untie his shoelaces.

Out of the corner of his eye, *a shadow moves across the floor*, blocking the moonlight in front of the window. His reflexes make him duck into the hallway, frozen against the wall.

He inches one eye back around the corner — *A LONG, DARK ANGULAR FACE*, unlike that of any creature he has ever seen, pulls away from the window. A jolt of adrenaline goes through him; he cannot move. He stays there, transfixed on the spot where the face was. He doesn't know what to do. He twists back into the hallway, leaning against the wall, the image of the long snout, deep eye sockets, skull-like, angled cheekbones, all covered by a midnight-black leathery hide, still seared into his mind.

In a daze, he wanders back down the hallway toward his room. From the doorway, he checks the bedroom window —*nothing*. His eyes remain seized on the window, as he makes his way to the foot of his bed. He pushes it, inch by inch, away from the window, until it is in the corner of the room. He then sits down on it, still watching the window…waiting.

The drizzle turns to rain — the rain to sheets.

The sound of his feet rubbing together, a mind of their own. Time starts to come back to him. His muscles begin to unstiffen; he lies back. His eyes remain on the window, but they are heavy, his mind worn — he sleeps.

Chapter 3
MUD

At school, students are settling in for roll call. Head down, Dusty shuffles through the noisy clatter to his desk and takes out his pencil. The moment Miss Gutierrez speaks, all conversation drops and the students fall into their chair-desks, as if a higher level of gravity has just been turned on by a switch.

After roll call, Miss Gutierrez starts in on her history lesson.

"How many of you have heard of Einstein?"

Dusty huddles lower over his desk as he draws.

"Right, most of you have, probably even those of you who didn't raise your hands have heard of him — you may not know a lot about him — you may not be able to answer any focused questions about him, but he is part...."

Sarah's hand shoots right back up in the air, eagerly waving about.

"Yes, Sarah...?"

"He was a scientist. He was one of the smartest of—of scientist. He made up E equals mc squared. The theory of relativity. And he was the best, even though, and greatest scientist ever and he — he had failed math, in like, grammar school."

"Ah! Thank you, Sarah. Very good: this is my point exactly. Some of what you said is true, but as I was going to say, Einstein as we, well, as the public know him, has become a bit of a myth. The story that he had failed math in school was indeed even taught to me in elementary school, but...in fact, it's not true. On the contrary, he always excelled in math, teaching himself ahead of his classmates by several years. History can be tricky. What we..."

Dusty pauses and leans back, absorbing the sketch on his desk from a different perspective. But it is not the familiar coyote that he has been working on. Today he has been etching something new: beside the coyote sketch is the dark, angular face from outside the window last night.

———

Later that day, the students are brought to the main school building.

The nurse is in her office, performing a scoliosis test as the rest of the students wait outside the door for their turn. Most of the kids have lunch boxes, as the students have been told to go straight to lunch when their turn is over. Dusty is the only one with a brown paper bag as a lunch box. He is now second in line, behind Hector. Megan is third. Miss Gutierrez is way back at the end of the line, talking with another teacher.

The nurse opens the door and Sarah waltzes out; grape-flavoring wafts after her, as she makes smacking noises with her gum. She whips her head from side to side in search of something, anything, worthy of her interest.

The nurse, a sturdy, hale woman, who from afar would be mistaken for an ancient Viking warrior, were it not for her olive skin, jet-black hair, magenta lips, and kind brown eyes, lowers her sight to the next child in line. "Hectooooor. You ready?"

She guides Hector in. As she is closing the door, she gives a quizzical look to Dusty.

Meanwhile, Sarah calls out toward Miss Gutierrez. "Miss G!"

Miss Gutierrez either doesn't hear her, or she is used to tuning kids out. Sarah tries again, increasing the volume, as if utterly unaware that Dusty and his eardrums are inches away. "MISS G!"

Megan chimes in. "You don't have to ask her! She said we could just go straight to lunch when we're done."

Sarah's gum smacking intensifies. "I know that, Megan! I'm not dense. That's not what I'm gonna ask her! Miss G!!"

Megan's cheeks turn ardent, rosy red. "What are you gonna ask her then?…"

Sarah ignores her.

Megan's not done. "You smell…dense."

«Right, Megan! That's makes a lot of sense! My God! MISS G!»

Dusty is fixed on the handle of the nurse's door. Grape flavoring! When is it going to move?

Sarah's yelling has finally become too piercing to ignore. Miss Gutierrez turns her head. "What!?...Is it...Sarah?"

Sarah heads over to Miss Gutierrez. Megan talks in Sarah's direction, but speaks to the world. "Makes perfect sense! It's so much bad smell packed into one area that it's dense!!"

Sarah doesn't hear; she has already started talking at Miss Gutierrez before reaching her. Megan gears up again. "SO MUCH BA....!"

The handle shoots down, the nurse's door swings open and the nurse interjects. "*A la!!* Keep it down! No!? Can't hear myself think."

Hector walks out. The nurse looks at Dusty, maintaining her expression of disbelief. She seems to be stuck like this. "I'm sorry; I don't remember meeting you. I'm Abigail."

Her expression stays the same, but her mouth moves like a puppet; her speech pattern sounds completely different than a moment ago. She extends her hand to shake. He extends his hand.

Behind him Megan blurts out: "You don't remember meeting him because he's new...it's pretty hard to remember meeting someone if they're not there for you to meet."

Abigail shakes his hand. He tries to do the same, but his rhythm is behind. She puts her hand on his shoulder and guides him in. Abigail stays at the door a moment looking at Megan — as if to say, "Little girl, what is wrong with you?" — before shutting the door behind her.

"What's your name?"

"Dustin."

"Dustin….» She lets the name hang in the air, mulling over how it sounds, as if she has never heard it before.

"Well it's good to meet you, Dustin…. So, you're new, huh? New ta town, or just here? Where you from?" Her speech patterns seem to come in waves, usually starting in a formal, business-like tone, before a more relaxed New Mexican accent creeps back in.

Dusty is looking around the room. It's small, and, despite being overcrowded, well-organized, adorned with creaky, old wooden furniture and outdated public service messages, anti-drug posters, and health and anatomy charts with curling edges and brittled texture from years of desert heat. The only recent artifacts in the office are a few drawings made by Dusty's classmates. He recognizes the drawings as the winning entries from a local government-sponsored contest. The three best posters advertising water conservation would win the artist a fifty dollar savings bond in their name, and their posters would be put on display, although it wasn't specified what or where "on display" meant...until now. Dusty's drawing had been of a man pensively staring into a toilet bowl. Below it read, "Each time you flush it uses five gallons of water." He wasn't one of the winners.

On the right side of the room is a single window a third of the way open, with thick, faux-wood blinds. He stares through the slits as the midday sun bakes last night's wet dirt into powder.

"Ok, Dustin...» The nurse interrupts, realizing she's lost his attention. He had almost forgotten she was there, hypnotized by the soft warm breeze moving through the window, delicately lifting the blinds for a moment before dropping them back against the window sill.

"Take your shirt off, ok? Look straight ahead at the wall here. Put your feet right here and here, and look straight ahead, right at that piece of tape on the wall here."

She demonstrates the feet position and points at the piece of tape as though she is going through a strange ritualistic dance.

"We're gonna check on you for scoliosis. Ok...? So, your shirt off then — that's ok?"

He takes off his shirt, keeping his brown paper lunch bag in his hand the whole while. She looks at him quizzically. "You can leave your lunch bag on the chair."

He places it on the ground next to his feet.

She raises her eyebrows. "Ok, then." And picks up a clipboard on the desk beside the door. "Just Dustin?"

"Yeah."

She was not expecting that response. She flips through her papers. "Why's that? You don't like your last name?"

"I don't know…."

He watches the blinds delicately lift up again, suspended for a moment before tapping back against the window.

She tries again. "Just Dustin?"

"Ok."

She is perplexed, but she moves on, shuffling through the papers on her clipboard until she finds what she was looking for. She stands up straight and walks around the back of him, checking his neck and shoulders. "Try to stay straight, *mi hijo*. Look at the tape there, on the wall, there."

He sees the blue tape on the wall; he looks around it, but for some reason very vital to him, he doesn't know why, he never looks directly at it. He straightens up a little.

"Ok. And go forward, put your head down like you are going to touch your feet, ok."

He leans forward and as he does, his spine tilts, crooked off to the left side. Abigail is shocked. She tries to remain professional. "Are you going straight down?… Even? Try to stay EVEN, on both sides."

He doesn't move. The curve is so severe. Finally, she can't help herself. "Are you messing with me?"

Still, he doesn't move.

She begins to feel bad for what she just said. She stumbles for the right words to apologize. But before she can, he straightens up like an arrow.
"*A la* — Come on now!" She takes another half look to make sure things are aligned. Struggling to regain her professional air — "You can't do that; you're gonna make me lose my mind here. It's hard trying to figure out…what lines up with…and whose body does — *ah!* You don't have to go and make it worse." She tries to sound stern, but she can't help but be relieved that the mood has been lightened.

Dusty's head is still upside down. He murmurs. "I'm sorry.…"

A slight grin creeps over the nurse's lips. "Oh… you're fine. Go on, get outta here…. Dustin, no name, from nowheres."

Dusty shuffles to the door; he thinks he might have a small grin on his face as well, but he is not certain. He touches his face…

Stepping out into the hallway, his path is immediately blocked. A different classroom of students is walking by, single file, past the door and snaking around to the end of the scoliosis test line. Dusty is trying to cut through, but he catches a glance of something that stops him in his tracks — scooting towards him in line is the trampoline girl.

As she approaches, she spots him staring at her. He looks down. As she passes by, she seems to hang there for a moment, but the line pulls her away. He watches her feet and legs as she drifts past.

Meanwhile, Megan is getting impatient — "'Scuse me…" —trying to shoo Dusty out of the way with the back of her hand, but before she knows it, he is gone, having already ducked through the line.

He can hear Abigail let out an audible sigh at the sight of Megan, as he heads off to lunch.

———

Later, Dusty sits in his large cottonwood tree, overlooking the school yard. He opens up his brown paper bag. Inside is a peanut butter sandwich on whole wheat bread, string cheese, a small bag of baby carrots, and an apple juice box.

He places each one on the tree limb in front of him as he watches the other kids play. When he gets to the juice box, he seems to have run out of level spots amongst the curves and knots of the tree branch, so he lays it on its side, where it teeters upon a large knot.

He reaches for his sandwich. As he does, the juice box falls off the limb — *down, down, down* — bouncing onto the ground. It is quickly forgotten as he looks back up over the school yard and bites into his sandwich, leaning back on the tree.

The students swarm about. Gabe walks over to Sarah and her group of friends as his buddies watch from a distance. He leans against the wall and talks with a huge grin on his face as he intermittently pops red dots of candy into his mouth.

In front of them a group of students play basketball, oblivious to the baking sun. To the left of that, others try to organize a kickball game, but the sport of it seems to lie in the politics of picking a team rather than in the kicking. Currently, Megan holds the ball — and with the ball, like a royal crown — comes the anxious attention of the other would-be kickballers.

Dusty has seen this fable play out before, and knows the bell will ring well before she is ready to surrender her pulpit; knowing this, Dusty looks away, wanting to find something new.

He does. Off to the side of the main school building, out of sight from the rest of the school, Dusty sees a group of five boys. Two of the boys (one significantly taller than the other) are facing each other. The other three boys crowd around the smaller boy, but he is not backing up. In fact, he is incrementally moving forward with a preternatural calm.

Suddenly, the larger boy clubs the smaller boy across the side of the head with his fist, knocking his head violently to one side. Nearly instantaneously, the smaller boy explodes toward the larger one.

Not expecting this burst of energy, the larger boy's legs go out from under him as the smaller boy tackles him to the ground, landing him flat on his back. The larger boy is in shock, but the smaller one has lost no focus or rage, and proceeds to bludgeon the face of the larger one. He does not get very far before the other three boys begin to kick and drub at his ribs and head, eventually pulling him off their large comrade and holding him to the ground.

The large boy stammers to his feet and christens the small boy with three hard stomps to the head. He huddles over the small boy's now limp body, spitting between bursts of words and gasping for breath; he then abruptly turns and walks away.

His comrades follow, an awkward mixture of adrenaline, confidence, and fear in their stride. The smaller boy is left where he lies. He's not moving.

Dusty scurries down from the tree.

In front of him is the swarming hive of students on the playground, buzzing around in the baking sun. He steps out of the shade and onto the playground, shielding his eyes from the harsh light with both hands. He tries to make his way to the other side while doing his best to avoid the frenzy, but the other students abruptly knock and step into him without even seeming to notice.

Finally, he makes his way into the sliver of shade along the main school building. Following it like a tight rope toward the side, he turns the corner. There lies the smaller boy.

The boy has blood on his face, some of which has dripped into the dust, forming a black mud that is already being soaked up by the same desert thirst that evaporated last night's rain fall.

Whimpering.

Dusty walks over and sits by him in the dirt. The mewling goes silent; the boy senses someone is there and flinches as if he might get hit again. After a few moments, he lifts his head and turns to see Dusty sitting off to the side.

The boy gets up, wiping the blood from his face with his shirt. His new purpose — avoidance — seems to have erased his pain. He glances at Dusty before disappearing around the corner. Dusty stays, sitting in the dirt.

The school bell rings. Lunch is over. Dusty lies back in the dirt and looks up at the sky.

A few sparse, puffy little clouds are stuck overhead. With no wind to carry them, they seem as if they are slowly starting to drift down to earth. The noise from the other students is nearly gone.

Dusty stands and walks out onto the basketball courts. He can see all the other kids and teachers filing into the classrooms in the distance. He keeps walking, but not toward them — toward the fence. He crawls underneath it.

He walks in the middle of the lonely dirt road, occasionally looking back, but there is no coyote. He wanders off the road, toward the hills, hiking upward.

After a while, he stops and props his back up against a piñon tree. Below, he can see the school. The brown adobe buildings and homes group together, marbled amongst the landscape, mixing with swirls of trees, rock, and dirt.

He continues up the hill, and each time he stops and turns to look back, everything below looks less and less real: a toy town. The trees and earth look like something out of a diorama. The few cars look like matchbox toys and the roads seem cartoonish as they wiggle through the terrain; only the arroyo seems real. With certainty and incontrovertible purpose, it slices through the middle, dividing the world.

He absentmindedly feels the ground with his fingers. He lifts a piece of dirt up. From here, the pebbles of dirt seem bigger than his house — bigger than the entire schoolyard — if he holds them closer.

He rubs the dirt into his hands until it looks like he's wearing brown gloves. And with his new set of hands, he starts back down the hill.

He explores past where he usually turns off to go to school, following the dirt road as it winds around to the other side of the arroyo, merging onto a less forgotten and wider dirt road.

As he walks, he slides his feet through the dust and stares down the long dirt driveways branching off to homes in the distance. To the right, they snake up into the hills, mysterious and superior; to the left, they slide down along the arroyo, cozy and whimsical.

Each driveway shares one thing in common: they are lined with handmade fences consisting of rusty barbwire strung between sticks of old piñon wood sticking up out of the dirt.

Dusty keeps walking, shuffling his feet in the dust, until he comes across one particularly inviting driveway, the only one without a fence. Tall wildflowers, weeds, and tire marks wind down to a two-story, light-beige adobe house, surrounded by trees. Poking out from behind the house, on the left is…the trampoline. There are no cars in the driveway.

The air is still and quiet.

He looks down the main road — still no cars coming from either side.

He descends along the driveway, keeping his head down, watching the dirt crunch and skid beneath his feet, occasionally peeking up at the tall weeds and wildflowers on either side. Before he knows it, he has arrived at the trampoline. He looks over at the house: it looks warm and calm. Inside, he imagines linen sheets on a large bed with a soft ray of sunlight warming a corner of the room.

He turns back to the trampoline. Most of it is covered in the shade of a few piñon trees.

He puts his hand on the black surface. The material feels cool and electric; the hairs raise up on his arm.

He pulls himself up, and as he does, he hears a pop as an electrical shock hits his arm. He grabs his arm, but after a second realizes it didn't really hurt.

He stands up, trying to find his balance on the buoyant surface. He tries to jump, but the surface gives downward along with the force of his legs and follows them right back up, leaving him standing right as he was before.

Well, that doesn't seem right, so he tries it again, but with more force; this time the surface goes down and comes right back up, also with more force, pushing his legs straight up into his chin and tossing him onto his butt.

He sits there for a second. He rubs his hands on the surface again until it lets out another pop. He springs to his feet again.

This time he jumps, but keeps his body stiff enough to absorb the trampoline's rebound force — and up he flies. He's got the hang of it — kind of.

He jumps. He keeps jumping, occasionally losing his balance, but bouncing right back up again. He keeps jumping. He jumps and jumps until his legs feel like noodles and his whole body feels like a rag.

He slinks off the trampoline and slips underneath it to rest in the cool, dark shade.

He is awakened by a ringing sound in the distance. He stays under the trampoline, watching the tiny sparkles of light sift throughout the trampoline's surface.

When discernment comes back to him, he recognizes the ringing. It's the school bell. He rolls out from under the trampoline and stands up, looking back toward the schoolyard. In the distance, he can see the trampoline girl and the younger girl who was with her on the trampoline last time racing each other home from school on the dirt road.

Dusty scrambles over the fence at the edge of the arroyo and climbs up a piñon tree growing on the slope. He settles midway up on a sturdy branch. He is about level with the trampoline from here and can see it clearly. It is only about forty feet away, but he is hidden by the other branches and the long dark shadows of the late day.

The trampoline girl and younger girl are almost at their driveway now. They scamper down, past the tall weeds and yellow wildflowers, into the house. Dusty can hear them stomping up the stairs and after a few moments, scampering back down — then busting out the back door. They take off their shoes and throw themselves on the trampoline, bouncing each other around, laughing, yelling and knocking each other over.

Behind them, an old white Pontiac van pulls into the driveway. The girls glance over at it and the little one jumps off the trampoline, puts her shoes on, and runs toward it. The trampoline girl sits down on the trampoline, watching as it rolls to a stop. The sound of the van door sliding open. A boy comes running out from behind the van. It's the same boy, a couple of years older than Dusty, who was jumping with the girls before. He runs right past the little girl, who instantly does an about-face and hurries after him.

She calls out behind him. "Nathan! Nathan!"

The boy drops his backpack on the ground and leaps straight onto the trampoline.

"Nathan, wait!" The little girl stops to remove her shoes before getting on the trampoline again. "Nathan!…"

In the background, a middle-aged lady gets out of the driver's side of the white van. She has black and silver hair, big round glasses, and a pleasant smile on her face. She walks around the van to the passenger side, returning into view with an elderly man. He is hunched over, his head stuck facing the ground; a few strands of dark hair are swept back against his shiny, sun-spotted head. He carries a cane as if it were a bodily extension. With her guidance and the assistance of his extra limb, they delicately make their way toward the house.

Meanwhile, Nathan is busy trying to time his jumps just right so he can send the trampoline girl flying off the trampoline.

"Nathan! Take off your shoes…Nathan…." The little girl continues to yell as she tugs and pushes at him.

A jumping frenzy ensues — Nathan chasing the trampoline girl, the little girl chasing Nathan, and the trampoline girl trying to be left alone — until the little girl can't keep up and loses her bearings, tumbling off the trampoline, falling chin first onto the hard ground.

Before she even has time to process the pain, she looks up at the other two, assessing their reactions. Her eyes begin to water and her face starts to crumple.

Nathan is watching, but this has not stopped him from jumping or chasing the trampoline girl, who has in fact stopped and is trying to see if her sister is ok. He lands on top of her, losing his balance, his legs toppling up in the air, flipping him onto his back. He yells out, "I hit you with my butt!" And, screeching with laughter, "I almost just broke my neck!"

Not getting the proper attention that she feels she deserves, the little girl begins to yell at the top of her lungs. The trampoline girl climbs down to her and quickly quiets her. "Sadie! Shhh. Mom won't let us jump anymore if she hears you crying. What's wrong?"

The little girl yells again at the top of her lungs. "Nathan!"

She forces herself to cry. The rapacious need, the desperation for attention, piping into the shrillness of her voice make it far more alarming and taxing to hear than the real thing.

Nathan finally rolls over and pops his head over the edge of the trampoline. She stops, waiting for his reaction. After a once over glance, he curtly decides — "You're fine, come on."

The trampoline girl tries to help Sadie to her feet.

"I am not fine." She refuses to stand up. "I broke something."

The trampoline girl finally gives up trying to help and they all just sit there for a while, staring at the ground.

Dusty has not moved an inch. He looks down at his hand on the branch. Surprised to see it there, he knows he is supposed to recognize it as his own, but it does not feel like him any more than the rest of the tree branch does.

Eventually, Sadie decides she is ok and wants to play again. But it is too late; the mood is dampened. No more jumping.

The girls sit on the trampoline, picking at the petals of a camphor weed. Nathan gets bored and goes back inside.

The sun continues to fall, stretching out the valleys of shade and highlighting dancing dust particles in the air. Details are crisp and sharp, the perfect amount of sunlight for the eye to absorb the contours and dimensions of the world around it. Dusty can see the few freckles on the trampoline girl's skin and a golden glow shining off her hair as she sits on the trampoline.

After a while, the girls get off the trampoline, put on their shoes, and gather their backpacks. The little girl heads back inside, but the trampoline girl pauses for a moment; she turns and looks up at the tree, staring right in Dusty's direction. Can she see him? He remains completely still — so does she, her gaze locked on his tree.

From the house, the little girl calls out to her sister, in a pining tone. "Come o-o-o-o-h-o-o-o-h-o-n!"

But the trampoline girl does not move. She keeps staring up at the tree, expressionless. Dusty can see straight into her eyes. He feels as if he should look away, but he doesn't. The color of her eyes is hidden by the rusty tint of the sun falling behind the hills. Everything about her looks golden brown. The shape of her eyes feels warm, frenetic, but calming at the same time.

The little girl's voice now comes sharp and short, as if she is mimicking an angry parent. "Time to go inside!!"

The gaze is cut. The trampoline girl finishes slinging her backpack over her shoulder and heads inside.

The back yard is quiet now. Dusty climbs down from the tree. He stands at the fence, staring into the yard. He looks up at the house. He can faintly hear the chatter of ebullient voices and the clanging of dishes.

After a moment, he climbs over the fence and lies down on the trampoline, looking up at the clouds, listening to the murmurs from inside the house.

He closes his eyes.

Gentle waves of cool air rhythmically cut through the warmth around him. His head and eyes feel heavy and dusty....

When he opens his eyes, it is dark. The air is much cooler and his body has stiffened, compressed, wrapping around itself for warmth. He no longer hears the murmur of voices from inside. As his senses come back to him, he becomes aware of a strange feeling in the air, like a thought that is not being expressed, or a noise that is not being heard.

He raises his head. Just outside the periphery of his vision, he can tell someone — or some*thing* — is standing between him and the house.

He forces the muscles of his neck against their will to look in its direction. There stands the trampoline girl, about ten feet away, staring directly at him. He quickly sits up.

They are both still. Her frenetic eyes look as if they are thinking a thousand things at once.

Dusty starts to climb off the trampoline.

"Do you want to jump?" she whispers.

He freezes, half off the trampoline. She begins to softy walk toward him. She climbs on to the trampoline. He stays frozen, half off, half on. She starts to jump. Nearly forgetting her whisper for a moment — "Come on."

He releases his grip on the metal edge of the trampoline and sits on the side, watching her. She stops and returns his look. She motions for him to join her.

He stands up and tries to remember what he had discovered from jumping earlier. It couldn't have been more than a few hours ago, but his mind will not let him think.

She bounces beside him with lithe ease, the wake of her jumps wobbling him about as he struggles to find his trampoline legs, stumbling forward, falling backward.

Amidst his chaotic effort, he notices a small smile on the trampoline girl's face. And, before he knows it, he has been launched into the air and comes careening down, nearly falling on top her. She dodges out of his way at the last minute, letting out a laugh. But next thing he knows, she swoops down from the sky, landing on top of him, retorting his accidental ambush with an intentional one.

They crash into one another, losing their balance, falling onto their backs; she rolls over on the trampoline, until her laughter fades. Dusty sits up.

Lying back, the trampoline girl props her torso up with her elbows.

The sound of wind rustles through the arroyo.

The murmur of voices is heard from inside again.

Suddenly, a booming voice from the house — "Hey!"

The trampoline girl gasps! And she springs upward as if being awakened by an alarm. She scrambles off the trampoline. Nathan is standing outside the front door, staring at them. She looks back, but Dusty has already scrambled over the fence and is looking back at her.

He disappears down into the arroyo.

Dusty catches his breath at the bottom. And, as his pulse starts to slow and the intoxication of the moment starts to fade, it suddenly dawns on him how late it is.

His pulse picks back up and he glides over rocks and dodges through the jagged turns of the arroyo as he hurries home.

Though the sun has long since fallen behind the mountains, the path is clearly lit, as the pale, still oddly bright moon illuminates the terrain. Up ahead, Dusty can faintly hear a voice calling out. He knows who it is — his gliding turns into a sprint.

Over big rocks and fallen branches, he hears the swift pitter-patter of his own feet, instinctively searching for smooth ground. Faster — until he can only hear the sound of the wind whizzing by his ears. Then —

"Dustin!!"

He is now close enough to make out the tone in his sister's voice. She sounds frantic and desperate. «Dustin!!»

She is on the other side of the house, calling out in any direction that she can.

He is almost there. The path turns.

Suddenly, the arroyo walls fill with the glow of flashing red and blue lights. He slows down, looking up. Police lights are seeping down through the brush from his house up above.

He scrambles to the edge of the arroyo, poised to begin the climb up to the house, but he does not move.

His body stiffens. His breath stops.

A figure stands in the middle of the arroyo, not twenty feet away from him.

His bones feel like they will shatter under the stiffness of his muscles. His heartbeat overloads and resets to zero.

There it stands, *the creature from outside the window last night.*

The dark angular features…

The moonlight sculpts every detail.

Sharp skeletal cheekbones and a muscled jaw lead down an elongated snout to a lion-like muzzle and nose. Sticking out of the top of the head are fur-covered ossicones, like a giraffe's, flanked by tall pointed ears. The bottom of its muzzle and top of its head are covered with slightly longer fur.

Also like a giraffe, a long but strong neck makes up nearly half its height — the height of a large man;

this neck leads down into a pair of long skeletal arms that would reach well past the ground if they were straightened, but they are not; they are bent significantly back behind its body, keeping the hands in proximity.

Those hands — the hands that Dusty saw out of his window — like enormous spider legs.

The creature's torso is mainly hidden by its large hind legs, like those of a kangaroo. Its powerful tail would also be like that of a kangaroo — were it not for one long stripe of fur on top — the same longer fur visible on the creature's head and muzzle.

Short midnight-colored fur, spotted with large, asymmetrical patches of deep, deep red, cover the creature's entire body — except for parts of the face, joints, and hands, where a tight black leathery hide is revealed.

Sweeps from the red and blue pulsating lights above are the only reminder that time itself has not ceased.

The creature does not move: it only stares, its dark, shadowy eyes hooded by its angular features. No light — not the flashing red and blue, nor the bright moonlight — seem to reflect even a glint of luminance off the matte black of the creature's eyes.

Directly behind the creature on the ground, there appears to be some kind of box or crate. And further down the arroyo, the tunnel emits the same strange amber glow that Dusty had found peculiar last night.

"Dustin!!"

A flashlight beam cuts down into the arroyo. Dusty's eyes dart over for a quick second; when he looks back, the creature has already begun making its way toward the tunnel in the distance. The crate that was behind it now appears to be strapped to its back.

The flashlight is coming closer.

The creature disappears into the amber glow of the tunnel.

"Dustin!"

Chapter 4
THE GLOW

His sister stands in front of the house, squeezing Dusty close, both arms locked around him, suffocating him in affection. Two police officers close the gate behind them on the way to their cruiser in the driveway. The moment they've left, his sister buckles into a frenzy, petting and kissing Dusty's head.

"Thank you. Thank you. God. Thank you… thank you…thank you."

And although Dusty can see what is happening and he can feel that his sister needs him to express something back…he is not sure how — or what to do.

"Where were you? The school said you were missing! They found your backpack there, but you were nowhere to be found. Oh my God! I can't believe you're here. Thank you, thank you. My God, where were you? I thought you were — I don't — where were you? But you're ok? I'm so…" She finally releases her breath with a deep sigh. "Where were you?"

She continues to hold him tight, rocking side to side with her head next to his.

She pulls back and looks at him. "Are you hungry? Come on, let's get you something to eat — and thirsty!? Where were you?"

She hurries him inside.

——

That night. Dusty is sitting up in bed, his eyes wide open. Bright moonlight is beaming in through the window, and the loud hum of silence is filling the room.

He gets up, gets dressed, and steps quietly through the hallway to the front door; he grabs his shoes and coat from the foyer closet, ties and buttons up, before snatching the flashlight off the window sill, where he left it last night. He goes outside, latching the front door silently behind him.

He circles around the house toward the arroyo. Once at its edge, he can still see the amber glow seeping from the tunnel below. He makes his way down.

As he gets closer, the cold white light of the arroyo's moonlit rocks is melted away by the alluring warmth of the tunnel's glow.

He peers inside. It is still too dim to see well. He turns on the flashlight. Water drips from the ceiling. The ground is a slush of twigs and pebbles, layered over hard cement. Up ahead, maybe sixty feet away, he can see where the tunnel opens back up on the other side. Halfway down, seeping out from a crack on the right side of the tunnel, is the source of the glow.

He crouches down and steps into the tunnel.

He can hear the textured echoes of every movement around him: the water dripping, the soft wind outside, whispering as it swirls by the entrance, the crunch of the twigs and pebbles beneath his feet.

Up ahead, Dusty can see that the glow is actually emanating from behind a circular metal hatch. It's slightly open. He turns the flashlight off and stuffs the handle end into his pocket. He tries to pull the hatch open further. It's heavy, but it slowly begins to budge. He guards himself behind it as it opens wide enough for him to peer in. Inside is a smaller tunnel, still cement, with a thin trail of water trickling down the middle; he cannot see where it ends. He pushes the hatch open further and crawls inside, following the glow.

He makes his way further and further into the tunnel, until it starts to curve slightly to the left. His knees are becoming tender against the cement.

He looks back, no longer able to see the hatch; it has disappeared behind the curve. The glow, however, is becoming more intense: it feels close. Up ahead, he can see that it is emanating from a dirt hole, freshly dug into the earth, which veers off to the left side, breaking through the cement wall, at a slight downward angle.

He looks inside. The air feels cold, thin, and musty. The richness of the amber seems to melt the contours of the dirt. The hole continues on, curving down to the right.

He crawls inside.

The dirt feels fresh and moist on his hands and stomach. He can see markings and scrapes that look like they were made by the hind paws and long hands of the creature.

The glow is getting brighter and the tunnel is getting narrower; he is starting to feel the snugness of the earth around him, and his flashlight digging into his side. It is too tight for him to turn around. *How did the creature fit through here?* Dusty pictures his sister's pet hamster, squeezing under the door when they lived in San Francisco. In order to get back out of this tunnel he would have to try to inch himself backward, pushing with his hands and pulling with his toes.

But the glow is beckoning him onward.

Just a little further, maybe.

He continues down.

Suddenly, the tunnel dead-ends into a circular stone door. Its center is engraved with what appears to be the imprint of a planet, which has an odd texture and bluish hue unlike any he has ever seen before. Behind it, the amber light is bright, beaming through the cracks all around the edge.

Carefully, he works his fingers into the crack, attempting to pull the door open, but it will not budge. He tries pushing on the edge — *nothing* — the other side — *nothing* — the top, the bottom — *nothing* — it will not budge. But there is light cutting through all the way around the circle. *Why won't it move?* He tries to look through the crack, but all he can see is amber — his eyes will not adjust.

He relents and lays his head down for a second, trying to catch his breath, but the snugness of the earth around him makes it difficult to breathe.

He stares at the door. At first, he had thought the engraving in the center of the door was a planet; however, as he lies there, looking at it, it looks more like the moon — but no — beyond its odd color, there is still something unfamiliar about it.

The stone of the door is finely porous, with glints of silver light that seem to flare up and die back down into blackness, over and over again.

He reaches out, touching the details of its porous surface; it feels as if it is crumbling apart, like a sand sculpture, but nothing is falling off — the structure of it remains the same. As he pulls his hand away, the silver glints of light all fade to hollow blackness. The door then slides backward, disappearing into the dirt.

Beaming amber light — he can barely see.

He crawls inside.

As he stands, he feels the flashlight squeeze out of his pocket and roll onto the floor. His eyes begin to adjust to the light and he finds himself inside a stone room, about thirty feet by thirty feet. The entire room is made of coarse rock, like an ancient Mayan temple. It appears to be empty.

Still stumbling for his footing, he gazes upward: moss and vines creep along the walls, leading all the way up and meeting at a point in the ceiling. The ceiling.... *It's the inside of a pyramid.* At the apex, in the middle, is the amber light — too bright to look at directly.

Once he reaches the center of the room, there is a sudden jolt. The ground makes a popping noise — as if a latch has been released beneath it. Suddenly, the air is filled with the rumbling sound of stone grinding against stone. The floor begins to drop.

Dusty tries to sprint back toward the tunnel, but the quaking ground knocks him off his feet. He grips onto the trembling stone beneath him as it continues its rapid descent. He watches as the tunnel he came in from and the amber light up above rise higher and higher, further and further away. Maybe he can still climb up the wall if the floor stops…but it won't.

The trembling of the ground subsides, only to be replaced with a precise and smooth purpose. Down and down it falls, until he feels like he is looking up through the inside of a hollowed-out skyscraper. *Faster and faster…*

Suddenly, three of the four walls are no longer continuing down with him. Only the wall opposite the tunnel he climbed in through remains. This single wall continues downward an uncanny length, as the ground drops lower and lower, faster and faster still. If he tried to touch it, the wall (a complete blur) would rip him to shreds from the sheer speed with which the ground is lowering alongside it. The other three walls have now been replaced with deep black space — and, as his eyes adjust — *stars.*

Billions of stars.

The ground starts to slow, trembling and rumbling again. He sees the flashlight bounce off the edge and float upward, disappearing above him as the floor lowers past it. As the trembling becomes more jarring, the descent slows to an eventual stop.

Still holding on to the ground, Dusty looks around. The remaining wall goes on for as far as he can see — up, left, and right — forever. He can no longer see where he came from, only deep space above him.

Slowly, he rises to his feet. He cautiously moves to the edge of the floor opposite the wall — now just a floating square sheet of stone.

He looks over the edge: infinite space, speckled with endless stars. They seem so close, almost as if he could jump out and grab them, or jump and swing from one to the next, but in the same thought they seem eternally far away, divided by unimaginable time and emptiness, only to be wondered about, never to be known.

Behind him, he hears the sound of stone moving again! He drops low and grabs the ground — but everything remains still…. He looks back. There, in the middle of the singular wall is another small round door, strikingly similar to the one he'd come in from before. This one is also engraved with a similar image of a planet, but the spots and craters look much more familiar, like the moon he is used to seeing. The door slides open, revealing another dirt tunnel.

Then, it is silent.

He relaxes and turns back to the edge of the floor, facing deep space.

No sound, only space.

He can't remember if he has ever experienced complete silence before. Usually there is a humming loudness to it— white noise — as his ears push and strain for something to hear, but this is truly — nothing. He thinks about how when he sleeps, the sounds around him often play a role in his dreams; he wonders if he could hear nothing, could smell nothing, and feel nothing, what would he dream?

He tries waving his hand over the edge. Nothing. If he stepped off, would he just float off like the flashlight? He sits down on the edge, dangling his legs in the nothingness and gazing outward. None of the stars seem the same distance away.

Never-ending depth and direction.

He notices his feet feel light. He looks down; his shoe laces are floating. He's always liked looking at his shoes. He doesn't know why, maybe the keen shape curving around the contours of his foot and their mixture of textures; he likes how they've always looked different, with a new crease or spot on them.

After a while, he looks back at the tunnel behind him…he has nowhere else to go….

He crawls in.

The tunnel is almost pitch black. It's narrow, but here he could contort himself to turn around if he wanted to. The ground feels spongy and soft. He shuffles ahead. It begins to curve upward. For a second he thinks of his flashlight, floating up into space. The only sound is the hypnotic rhythm of his shifting limbs — his right side, his left side, his right side, his left side — sliding over the mossy ground, like the sound of a slowly sweeping broom.

The upward slope begins to level off. Then, it abruptly drops. He begins to slide head first, quickly gathering momentum — trying to slow himself — but it is too late: sudden, thrashing, impact. His arms buckle, cracking his head.

Wrapping his throbbing head and neck with equally throbbing hands and arms, he opens one eye to study his assailant: a boulder — blocking the tunnel. There is no imprint or design to it; it's just a simple, large, unshaped rock, blocking the passageway.

A dim, amber light shines through the sides.

He pushes with his still numb arms —*nothing.* He leans into it with his shoulder and pushes with his whole body. His feet begin to slide from the friction, but even so, it's working; it begins to tilt back. He gives one last heave and collapses. The mighty stone hangs, teetering in limbo before wobbling backward and coming to a rest, leaving the tunnel half open.

Chapter 5
THE DYING SUN

Dusty pokes his head out. He squeezes by the boulder, stepping down. The ground is spongy and covered with the same moss-like vegetation from the tunnel, but twice as thick. And thin, long vines that seem to have no end or beginning, spread like veins along the ground. He is having difficulty making out their color — or the color of anything in this light. Everything is tinted with the same deep and strange amber glow as before.

He looks up. The sky is cloaked in a dark mist that grows denser as it progresses upward — an opaque fog that stretches on endlessly, like a ceiling over the land.

To Dusty's right is a thick jungle, covered by a different breed of vines, — scaly — and several feet thick, wrapping themselves around enormous, rubbery, wet trees with massive thorns and monstrous leaves, the size of cars — all fighting for space among the impossible density of the dark jungle. Under each dark shadow cast by the gigantic leaves, there is curious rhythmic movement: the pulsating and swarming of hundreds of thousands of unknown critters. The festering forest extends thousands of feet upward, disappearing far above into the fog.

Off to his left, Dusty can see a valley enveloped in a blanket of moss and sporadically spread spherical shrubs, fuzzy and iridescent, like enlarged dandelion seed heads — about five feet in diameter. The thinner vines on the ground branch off into the valley, slithering along the landscape and dispersing, thinner and thinner, the further they are away from the dense jungle.

In the distance, the valley swoops up to a hill, on the side of which appears to be a single, small dwelling — a hut — with a pale blue light emanating from inside.

Dusty sets off toward the hut, entering the valley. As he walks, the vines slowly move out of his way to avoid being trampled, seemingly sensing his steps before his foot hits the ground. At that moment, he hears an odd, squeaky cry. He stops to listen — but finds he can no longer hear it — only the organic sounds of the earth and vegetation, slowly shifting.

Then — once again — "Squeak!" — like the cry of a bear, but miniaturized until it becomes high pitched.

Again!

It's coming from very close. *Down. To the right. At his hip.*

There is a small creature standing on the stem of one of the giant dandelion shrubs. He kneels down to look at it. It looks like a fossa, but it is no bigger than a grasshopper. It glares at him, poised to strike, as if unaware of its own size. It squeaks out another "roar."

Just then, Dusty feels something on his leg. He jumps. In the short amount of time that he's been standing still, the vines have begun to softly wrap themselves around his leg. He shakes his leg; the vines begin to retreat at the first sign of movement. He looks back at the tiny fossa, but it's gone.

He continues through the valley toward the hut on the hill. As he does, it becomes clear that when he had first come out of the tunnel, his view had been blocked by a portion of the dense jungle. Now, ahead of him, a vast landscape is revealed. He can now see that behind the hill are more hills — which in the distance are covered with buildings of a similar style to the hut, but bigger and grouped close together — hundreds of them — faint blue lights strewn across the hills — a town. The hills, gently rolling at first, rise higher further in the distance, toward a great mountain, at the top of which sits an ominous temple, hovering over the land, its blocks of massive, gloomy stone pyramiding up into the fog.

On the horizon, Dusty can now see the source of the dim glow that lights this world: between the hut and the mountain rests an amber dot, a fading sun, half-hidden in fog.

Dusty continues up the hill toward the hut. The terrain here is camouflaged by a thick overgrowth of plants that resemble giant pale fluffy feathers sprouting out of the ground. They come up to Dusty's hip, delicately drifting back and forth, responsive to the slightest breeze or displacement in the air.

This dwelling appears to be the only building nearby, peculiarly isolated from the town beyond it. As he gets closer, he can hear noises coming from inside, a series of different patterns, textured with enunciations, like muffled speech: among them, the whine of an animal — but calm, with a sleepy, humming quality.

There is a round window with open slats made from the same dry and stringy plant material as the rest of the hut. Up close the material looks crunchy, burnt and fragile, as if it would fall apart if he gripped it.

He hears shifting movement inside. He creeps up beneath the window, placing his hands on the side of the hut. It feels rough and sandy, and despite its weak appearance, the material is solid and sturdy.

He rises up on his tiptoes to look in.

Inside, only a few feet away, stands the creature from the arroyo, its giraffe-like neck and kangaroo-like body bending over as it reaches down to the floor. Its long skeletal arms and enormous raw-boned hands raise back up, holding a smaller creature, about a fifth the size. This babyish creature has huge eyes that take up most of its face, and immense bat-like ears.

Though its neck is similar in shape to the larger creature's, it is not as long proportionately. Its legs are similar to the larger creature's as well, but its tail is fluffy and light, like a squirrel's. The arms are shorter and fuzzy, with long brittle-looking fingers, like an aye-aye's arms and hands.

The larger creature places the smaller creature on its back, but the little one wastes no time in climbing upward, along the larger creature's giraffe-like neck toward its angular lion-like head. While this is happening, the larger creature walks away from the window, toward the other side of the room.

Dusty can see their habitation is lit by three pale blue fires, one on each of the three visible walls. Held in cups of dull crystal, they burn like lamps, midnight blue rocks at the center of the fuel source.

The corners of the room are overflowing with endless knickknacks, spreading up onto the walls, pinned up everywhere: tools, perhaps — or possibly toys, art…or weapons. Despite the clutter, everything seems to have its place. In the middle of the left wall there is a hallway leading into more of the dwelling; considering the hut is situated on the side of the hill, this hallway must lead into the hillside itself.

The creature, having now reached the other side of the room, approaches a bulky stone kettle with a blue flame writhing underneath it and steam rising from within. Inside it, vines, still alive, grip onto the rim of the kettle, trying to creep their way out.

The creature grabs a long knotted stick off one of the numerous shelves built into the wall near the kettle, and begins to stir, scraping the vines off the edge and pushing them back into the stew. They wrap themselves around the stick as the creature continues to stir.

Meanwhile, the baby creature makes its way to the hair-covered ossicones atop the large creature's head and grabs onto them, yanking from side to side. The larger creature lets out an annoyed moan.

At that moment, from the hallway, another creature enters; it snatches the baby creature off the head of the larger one, then helps it to the ground. This creature is half a foot shorter than the larger creature and shares many of the characteristics of the baby creature. It has huge round tarsier-like eyes and big bat-like ears, graceful arms, and strange hands with thin, delicate aye-aye-like fingers; its body resembles a poised cat that was meant to stand upright, along with a squirrel-like tail.

Suddenly, a strange guttural noise, similar to a foghorn, goes bellowing across the entire land. Alarmed, Dusty ducks down beneath the window, his ears ringing.

The sound fades, but there is still a slight tremor in the ground. This too subsides, and once again the air is quiet and still.

The hut is quiet, too: Dusty hears no murmur, no movement — not a creak.

He tries to match the stillness around him.

He feels like the only living thing left, except for whatever made that grim noise. His breath and heartbeat feel loud and boisterous like engines, betraying their own survival instincts. Surely it must hear him.

Then, once again, the strange guttural noise bellows across the land, rumbling the ground beneath Dusty's hands and feet. This time, Dusty can tell that the sound must be coming from further away than he had thought.

Sounds of movement suddenly return to the hut.

Dusty slowly rises back up to the window. *What are they doing in there?* The larger creature pulls a chain on the right side of the hut. Part of the wall swings down and a door, acting as a ramp, falls open.

They're coming outside!

Quickly, Dusty scurries, backing away from the hut, and drops inside the feather-like foliage a few yards away.

Once outside, the larger creature picks up the baby creature and turns right back toward the hut, climbing up a ladder built into the side and up onto the roof. The aye-aye/cat-like creature follows them up. They stand there, at the top, staring off toward the horizon, barely moving, their gaze fixed upon the dark, looming pyramid temple atop the mountain, and the fading amber sun setting behind it. The sun is nearly gone now; only a sliver remains.

It's somber and quiet again.

The setting sun reminds Dusty of home. He thinks of falling asleep on the trampoline at dusk and the trampoline girl being there when he woke up, the warm light wrapping around her and flitting through her hair.

He glances over his shoulder toward the valley, trying to distinguish where he came from, trying to spot the tunnel.

Just then, a deep red light begins to shine over the land.

He turns around. It's coming from the temple. The blood red light beams out from the very top of the pyramid, tinting the entire world; and then, after a moment, it begins to die back down, finally fading away. At that moment, the amber sun begins to slowly rise back up into the sky, reversing from the direction in which it was setting.

The creatures watch intently. The aye-aye/cat reaches over and takes the small creature from the larger creature, holding it tight. The larger creature puts its skeletal arm around the aye-aye/cat...and hangs its head.

After a while, another deep red light pulses from the temple again, lingering and penetrating the land as before. It slowly fades and then, once more, the curious amber sun rises a little higher into the sky.

Dusty feels something on his arm. He looks down. The vines have begun to wrap themselves around him. Instinctively, he tries to stand, but realizes that he will be seen by the creatures if he does so. Fighting his physical reaction, he crouches right back down. Thankfully, the vines retreat from this slight movement, slinking back into the earth — for now.

He looks back up at the amber sun; it appears to have stopped its ascension about fifteen degrees above the horizon.

Then — a third light from the temple — but this time the amber sun remains still, refusing to rise any further.

As the redness fades, the creatures solemnly climb back down from the roof.

Once the baby creature is put on the ground, it starts bouncing and frolicking about, blissfully unaware of the dark mood hanging over its elders, who watch by the hut door.

It's bouncing in Dusty's direction!

Dusty ducks even lower, tensing up. He can't see anything now, but he can hear it hopping closer. He tries to remain completely still, holding his breath. The vines, taking advantage of his stillness, begin to wrap around him again.

The little creature comes closer still.

Through the leaves he can see its head: it's only a few yards away…it stops…perking its enormous ears.

The vines are tightening around him, callously cutting off his circulation, like snakes enveloping their prey. He tries to remain still, but his skin begins to burn under their twisting friction and increasing strength.

The baby creature lifts its nose, sniffing the air.

Dusty can't hold his breath much longer; he is suffocating inside and out.

Just then, the larger creature lets out a calling moan. The baby creature instantly turns back and begins bouncing toward the hut.

Dusty gasps for air as quietly as he can, pulling at the vines, which release their grip automatically upon sensing his movement.

A sudden, fiery pain jolts through his right arm. He tries to hold back, but it is too late; his reflexes have already betrayed him — he has yelped out. The creatures must have heard him.

He looks down and reaches for his right arm. The insect-sized fossa-like creature that he had seen earlier scurries off his forearm, narrowly escaping his instinctive slap. The sharp pain remains, pressing unrelentingly at the nerve signals to his brain.

On the inner side of his right forearm, a bite mark begins to swell. His whole arm is throbbing, and so is his head. Nausea washes over him like a drug, and he breaks into a chilling sweat.

He feels a presence in front of him. He slowly raises his head. The large creature is standing over him. He tries to move, but he can't feel his legs. Fighting to stay conscious, waves of nausea and drowsiness bearing over him, he passes out.

Chapter 6
THE TRAIN

Dusty wakes up. He recognizes the burnt, brittle-looking wood on the ceiling; he is inside the hut. He is lying down, his torso and head propped slightly up. He looks down; the silk-like ends of the giant dandelion seeds have been intricately woven together to create a textured, but supple pillowy bed. He struggles to keep his eyelids open.

He hears soft rustling movements close by, down by his side. He tries to turn and look, but his head feels as though it is made of solid iron. Somehow he manages to shift his neck over just far enough to see: there, by the side of the bed, is the baby creature, staring up at him with its prodigious eyes — each eyeball is nearly the size of Dusty's hand — open wide, unblinking, unmoving.

Fighting to stay conscious, Dusty tries to scan the rest of the hut. On the other side of the room he can see the large creature. It is near the kettle, grinding a pale root-like plant on a stone slab.

Bringing his dreary gaze forward, he sees at the foot of the bed sits the aye-aye/cat, rocking back and forth, its enormous eyes muted by narrowed eyelids and a look of uncertainty and concern furrowed into the smooth fur of its brow. It shifts its gaze away, noticing Dusty's returned inspection.

Dusty tries to sit up, but he is too weak and too woozy. There seems to be a loss of connection between his body and mind. Even the slightest movement of his fingers takes a toll, a long and desperate journey between the thought and withered action.

Meanwhile, the large creature finishes grinding the root and makes its way toward him, scooting the baby creature over and taking its place, directly beside Dusty. It leans in close, examining him. He can now truly see the creature's eyes for the first time, hidden deep within its angular bone structure: matte black, glintless, seemingly sharp and angular themselves, unrelenting and powerful — and though they seem focused and intense, there is something comforting about them, something that appeals to Dusty's very nature — familiar, as if he has always known them without having seen them before.

The creature reaches down to Dusty's arm and applies the paste from the ground root to the bite mark. Then, the creature wraps the wound tightly in a sticky thin bark. It feels warm at first, then cool, and then oscillates back and forth. Warming. Cooling.

The large creature picks up the baby creature, placing it on its back. The baby wraps around the base of the large creature's long neck, like a koala hanging off a tree. The family of creatures all sit there, watching him.

The large one speaks to the aye-aye/cat in their strange humming dialect. The aye-aye/cat rises and walks over to the kettle, then returns with a stone bowl full of stew. Taking the bowl from the aye-aye/cat, the large creature offers it up, holding it in front of Dusty's mouth. It has a bitter, sandy smell, not unpleasant, but it does not trigger any appetite; Dusty is not thinking of food — he can barely think at all.

Noting Dusty's lack of appetite, the large creature gives the untouched stew back to the aye-aye/cat, who holds it with both hands, brow still slightly furrowed, studying Dusty with its wondrous eyes.

As the bandage continues to gently oscillate between warm and cool, consciousness begins to fade... dozing off...half asleep — *is the large creature talking to him?* It appears to be trying to tell him something now, motioning toward its chest. In a scratchy sounding voice, as if it is trying to imitate another language, it says, *"Scrak…cgule."*

Dusty's mind drifts to the moment when he first saw the creature clearly in the arroyo. He feels as if he is there again…

…outside his body, floating like wind through the crevices of the limestone and sand…

…twisting with the flashing of blue and red lights from the police car, up above his house.

Himself…and…"Scraggle" — standing — motionless…

…moving like a point through frozen time.

He can no longer keep conscious.

———

Dusty is awoken by a loud thumping noise at the entrance to the hut. His eyes are barely open before he is crowded by Scraggle and the Aye-aye cat, whispering to one another with an alerted urgency. Dusty can sense something is wrong, but he cannot move; he feels no better than when he fell asleep, but how long ago was that? Maybe only a few seconds, maybe hours — it couldn't have been days...could it?

A high-pitched squeal, like the agitated moan of a killer whale echoing up from the depths, calls from outside the hut door, followed by a haunting clicking noise — organic, but callous — like the crackle of feeding insects.

The Aye-aye cat grabs the Baby creature and they disappear into the hallway that leads into the hillside.

Scraggle watches them leave.

When they are safely out of sight, Scraggle picks up Dusty and carries him toward the kitchen on the other side of the hut. Scraggle lifts the lid off the kettle and gently puts Dusty inside, setting him in the puddle of what is left of the stew.

Dusty's vision is still blurry from sleep and his body is still too feeble to move, but even if he could, he's not sure where he would go. He struggles to breathe. His lungs cannot take in more than a few inches of breath at a time, but his struggle seems to bring a wave of consciousness with it: his vision clears, his senses fully awaken — but this only seems to highlight the disconnect between his mind and still incapacitated body.

The stew puddle feels lukewarm. The few vines left in the puddle of stew are wilted and lifeless. He looks down at his arm; the moisture from the stew is causing his bandage to wilt and peel off; he can see the bite mark has turned into a dark discoloration and has spread over his entire forearm, but before he can examine it further, a shadow blocks the light. He looks up; Scraggle is putting the kettle lid over his head.

It's dark — wait — there is light coming in from the holes where the handles punch into the kettle's brim. Struggling and mustering all the energy he can, Dusty inches over, trying to position himself so that he can peep out. As he tries to worm his unresponsive body closer, he hears the hut door swing open. The sound of hard and pointed steps thwack the floor, like pickaxes being swung into the wood. The strange, whale-like moan and clicking noise magnify.

Dusty finally manages to inch his face close enough to peer out one of the handle's holes. He can see the back of what looks like a giant man-sized insect. It stands upright, but its body continues down onto the ground, a tail with legs, like a lobster. There appears to be an inner body, hidden underneath the armor-like exoskeleton. Dusty cannot see its face, but a collection of antennae or feelers arch above and around its head, like a hood. It appears to be holding a staff or spear with a sharp and shiny crooked-shaped point.

The insect-like creature crowds Scraggle in a demanding way, pounding its spear on the ground as it hovers over him. But Scraggle seems calm, and starts moving over toward the kitchen — directly for the kettle.

Dusty can no longer see him, but can hear his movement right above the lid, crashing and clanging about.

After a few moments, Scraggle moves back over to the giant insect-like creature, with something under his long skeletal arm. Dusty recognizes it; it's the same crate that Scraggle had strapped to his back when Dusty saw him in the arroyo. Scraggle opens the crate, presenting what is inside it to the giant insect. The giant insect's arm extends; it has the shape of a praying mantis arm, but its texture and the shape of the hand more closely resemble that of a sloth or mole, with long translucent nails. Out of the crate it pulls what appears to be a plain old garter snake. The giant insect hands it away, out the door, but Dusty cannot see to whom.

Scraggle nods, as if he expects the uninvited guest to now leave. He walks the crate back over to the kitchen area, shuffling it back in the cabinets above Dusty's head. But the giant insect does not leave.

It turns toward the kitchen, revealing its head — clammy and pale. It has small beady eyes (hiding behind a murky film) — one on either side of a flat-boned, horizontal strip of a head, and a mouth — which appears to cut into its neck, like a hammerhead shark. Its numerous tiny jagged teeth show as it speaks

— in a moaning, ghastly voice — as the antennae tap the armor of its body, making a clicking noise accenting its unsettling tone.

It gestures toward the hallway, where the Aye-aye cat and Baby creature went, and begins to lurk inside. Scraggle follows with deft movement.

Dusty can hear the distinctive humming noises of the Aye-aye cat and the shrill moan of the giant insect, but when Scraggle enters, the noises are cut short. Moments later, the giant insect walks out of the hallway, Scraggle's large, powerful hand on the giant insect's back, calmly and politely guiding him toward the hut's exit. Nearly out the door, the giant insect pauses a moment, then turns back and gestures with its sloth-like hand toward its mouth, then moans and points toward the kettle.

Scraggle speaks back, waving his hand and shaking his head, as if to kindly deny. But the giant insect raises its head, sniffing with the slits of its nostrils at the air; it persists, moving closer to the kitchen. Scraggle backs up, slowly positioning himself between the giant insect and the kettle. The giant insect moves closer still, the hard-punching impact of its pickaxe-like legs on the floor, shaking the ground. The giant insect tries to push Scraggle aside, but Scraggle holds his ground, undaunted.

The giant insect turns its head to the hut entrance and lets out a hideous moan; three more giant insect creatures enter the hut, their numerous legs punching at the floor. The little hut shakes like a leaf. Then, a giant *crash!* Something falls from the shelves up above, smashing down onto the kettle. The lid is knocked loose and slides off, crashing onto the floor, leaving Dusty in plain view.

The head giant insect steps back and lets out a horrid *hiss*. Dusty is hit with the rank odor of its acrid breath, making it difficult to breathe; every inhale is cut short as his reflexes reject the rancid air. The other three giant insects crowd around to get a good look, but they keep their distance.

Where is Scraggle? Dusty can no longer see him.

The giant insects stare.

Dusty can feel their eyes on him, but he does not look up.

They just stand there, studying him.

As he lies there, his limp body and his head against the kettle, he studies the texture of the stone material it's made of. From up close, the little bumps on the surface look like vast mountain ranges, between deep valleys and twisting canyons, but there are no signs of life. He looks closer, squints…or are there?

Finally, the head giant insect pokes the kettle, leaving it rocking back and forth. After a moment, it backs away and signals to the giant insect on his left, which leaves the hut. The other giant insects do not move — they stay there, the room full of them — as others have entered, silently watching.

Dusty can feel a salty and metallic saliva building in his mouth; he swallows. It seems like a long time ago, but he remembers the taste well. When he was younger he had stomach problems and when he was taken to department stores he would often feel nauseous; he'd crawl inside the circles of hanging clothes and hide, trying to hold back the feeling of throwing up.

The one giant insect returns, bearing a large crate, similar to the one the garter snake was in, but at least four times the size. Holding the crate high, it creeps toward the kettle. On the head giant insect's signal, it darts forward, slamming the crate on top of the kettle. Dusty looks up at the crate above him. Suddenly, he is toppled over as the kettle is knocked backwards, then lifted and turned upside down. He falls out of the kettle; his limp body, with no reflexive muscles to protect it, slumps gruesomely into the crate — making a thick crunching noise as he lands.

Did his bones break?

He feels nothing, but almost wishes he could; at least then the pain would give him an idea of the damage, something to push and hope against, but now he has nothing to temper his paranoia — the grisly possibilities stabbing at his mind.

Knocking the kettle aside with its powerful lobster-like tail, the head giant insect anxiously shuts the crate door and uses the oddly-shaped tip of its spear like a key to lock the top of it shut.

Dusty continues to try to sense how badly ruptured his flesh and injured his bones must be, but there is no feeling —only the dull state of disconnect from his own physicality. His eyes seem to be the only thing left that are his own. From the inside, he can see that the crate is perforated like a sieve. He watches as they lift the crate, carrying him to the door. As they leave, Dusty's eyes scan the hut, but there is no Baby creature, no Aye-aye cat — and no Scraggle.

As the giant insects carry him outside, Dusty sees there is a wagon with an empty spot for his crate. In front of it, Dusty can see another wagon and crate. Inside it is the garter snake. And there are more wagons and crates ahead of that, a train of wagons and crates continuing on and on, further and further than he can see, in either direction.

From inside the hut, a sudden clatter of spiking giant insect steps, moans, frenetic clicking, hissing, and a series of loud thuds.

A single howl cuts through the racket, a familiar tone —*Scraggle.*

Dusty fights to lift his heavy head, but his view is blocked by the torso of the giant insect carrying his crate, its festering feelers clicking in between its thin, gummy inner body and its thick and slimy lobster-like armor.

The giant insect drops the crate hard on the wagon, Dusty's head hits.

Black.

Chapter 7
THE TEMPLE

Dusty opens one eye. The other half of his face is against the ground. He is still in the crate, but he doesn't appear to be moving. He shifts his eyes forward. The garter snake is still in its crate in front of him, but slightly higher up, a slight step above; they are no longer on a wagon.

He tries lifting his head — it works!

He has never had such an appreciation for the responsiveness of his own body. He tries to sit up — it's working — but his relief is quickly dampened as he experiences how little control he actually has; his arms feel full of sand — like iron weights — his legs are utterly unresponsive, and he still has very little feeling in his body. His instincts tells him to visually assess the damage, to look down and inspect the ruin brought upon his flesh by his violent fall from the kettle into the cage, but he rejects the thought; he doesn't want to look. Instead, he props himself against the side of his cage and looks around.

Behind him, a step below, is another cage. And taking up nearly every square inch of it is a creature with long white hair covering its large oblong body. It lies stock-still, a lump. It must be dead — no — it's breathing — with long, long pauses — between breaths. Dusty cannot see its head; perhaps the creature is in the fetal position and the head is tucked in away from Dusty's view, but for all he knows, it doesn't have a head. *Maybe that's all the thing is — an oval lump of fur.*

Dusty peers past the creature's cage, trying to make out the rest of the room in the dim light. *Where is he?* An enormous stone hallway, steadily curving up to the left, but their cages are not on the stone. They are leveled off on a strip of shallow steps made from the same brittle-looking — yet surprisingly durable — material as the hut, each cage placed on its own step as they line up the right side of the hallway. The wall on the opposite side of the hallway must be fifty feet away. The ceiling is equally as high as the hallway is wide and along it travels a strange vapor: a layer of smoke or fog, kinetic and billowing, flowing like a river above them. Dark clouds, continually reshape and fold outward, giving off a pale electric glow, as small sparks of lightning strike within them, like a miniature storm.

Dusty can feel his arm itching where the bite mark must be; it's begging him to look down. In some ways, it's a relief to have a sensation connecting him to his own body, but the reason for the connection leaves him with a hollow feeling, and the idea of looking down at his marred body fills him with disdain.

At that moment, noises echo from down the giant hallway, clacking and clicking. Monstrous shadows grow higher and higher on the walls as the clamor grows closer. Two silhouettes begin to take shape. Giant insect guards make their way up the hallway, long spears in hand.

Dusty slumps back down, pretending to be asleep. Their punching footsteps grow closer…

…closer…

…now, by his head…

…further…

…further…

Dusty lifts his head again, watching as they march away, up and to the left, until their shadows disappear out of sight.

Dusty looks around his cage. He remembers them closing the cage and twisting a knob on top with the spear to lock it. He can see the knob up there, but the crate is too tightly woven, the sieve holes too small to fit anything through. He tries lifting his arms, hoping to push against the crate; they move, but it is as if he is stuck in slow motion. Oddly, he is able to gather far more strength in his right arm, the bitten arm. Perhaps it is because when he was dropped into the crate, he landed on his left side — but perhaps not.

He lifts the bitten arm above his head, pressing against the crate. He can now see that the dark discoloration from the bite has spread over most of the arm and down onto his hand. The arm throbs with a jarring pulse, as if it has a separate heart, all its own. But he is still weak, and, no matter how great his mental effort, he still feels as though he is stuck inside an infantile body.

Down the line, he can see a fellow caged creature struggling to break out of its crate. It uses its ram-like horns and gorilla-like limbs — kicking, punching, frantically flailing. The crate gives and stretches just enough to absorb the power of the animal, rendering its attempts futile — an impossibly durable, tightly woven prison — like a silkworm's web. The creature collapses, gasping for air.

Dusty lowers his arm and looks down at the crate floor, where his head lay moments ago. How long was he asleep this time?

He looks back at his bitten arm; it continues to throb. The actual bite injury has nearly disappeared, but the discoloration seems to multiply every time he looks. He begins to pull his sleeve up to see how far it has truly spread. He freezes...

...movement coming from down the hallway...

Another long shadow is creeping up the walls, but this time it is silent. There is no clicking sound, no punching footsteps. This stealthy shadow is alone, and, as it begins to take shape against the wall, its angular features are undeniably familiar — *Scraggle.*

Scraggle is checking the cages as he stealthily sneaks through the enormous hall.

Dusty opens his mouth to call to him, but stops himself. He does not want the giant insect guards to hear him, so he tries to sit up, leaning closer to the side of the cage to keep Scraggle in his sight as he comes closer.

Scraggle has something in his hand. Dusty squints his eyes to see; it looks like a small knife.

He's almost here.

Scraggle sees him.

Scraggle wastes no time. He goes right for the lock on top of Dusty's cage; using the shiv, he tries to loosen it, but each time the lock begins to twist, the shiv slips out. Dusty sees dark maroon droplets falling toward him from above. The slipping shiv must be slicing at Scaggle's long fingers, making him bleed. But when Dusty looks at Scraggle's expression, there is no sign of pain, only intent focus.

Click!

Scraggle's got it; he pops the cage open.

Dusty tries to stand; having momentarily forgotten about his legs, he collapses onto his chin. Scraggle is already reaching into the cage. The long skeletal arms that had once seemed so alarming are now fond and familiar, comforting. Scraggle lifts him, slumping him over his back and moving back down the hallway from where he came.

Just then, a deafening moan undulates up through the ground, into the air, and into every fiber in Dusty's body, rattling his brain, numbing his every sense.

When it relents, Dusty finds himself on the floor, Scraggle shaken to the ground in front of him.

As the caged creatures against the wall begin to recover from the tremor, some start to howl, bark, yell, and fidget, losing their wits in tantrums of panic. Others become passive, their eyes wide and still with fear.

Dusty remembers that sound. It is the same foghorn-like noise that he had heard outside the hut, which had prompted Scraggle and his family to watch the dying sun from their rooftop. But now Scraggle and he are intimately close to its source.

Scraggle regains his footing, lifting Dusty back up onto his back, but does not continue down the hallway. Instead, he seems unsure of what to do. His long, regal, pointed ears twitch. He must hear something that Dusty cannot. He reluctantly turns around, taking them back up the hallway from where they came.

Up and up they go. Dusty can now hear a faint rumbling from down the hallway behind them. Gradually, the sound intensifies, coming closer, becoming more distinct. The sound of a thousand pickaxes swinging to the ground all at once — *the giant insect guards*. Dusty can see their shadows marching closer on the wall behind them. Scraggle puts everything he has into charging upward, trying to outrun them, but Dusty can feel that his limp weight is a burden — and, despite Scraggle's efforts — the ominous shadows are steadily gaining.

The thunderous guttural moan pierces the air again.

Scraggle is prepared this time, quickly grabbing the wall for support.

All consuming noise — rattling and disorienting every cell in the brain.

When his senses begin to return, Dusty sees that Scraggle is still holding onto the wall, struggling to find his bearings. The giant insects must have paused along with them; their shadows remain the same distance away.

Finding his footing, Scraggle continues upward. The grade begins to level off. Dusty tries to see up ahead; the dim amber glow is brighter and it looks as if the hallway opens up into a massive room: the top of the temple.

Scraggle stops, avoiding entering the massive chamber, staying in the hallway, hiding against the left wall, and peeking his head around into the room. Down the hallway, the shadows begin to close in. Dusty can see a spear poking around the curve.

The shadows are about to appear in the flesh.

At the last second, Scraggle darts across to the right side of the hallway, ducking himself and Dusty behind the crates, then sneaking up along the right wall as it hooks around into a forgotten corner of the vast room. There they hide, shrouded in shadow.

For a moment, everything is still.

Dusty can feel Scraggle's deep breaths and powerful heartbeat.

Scraggle takes Dusty off his back and sets him down against the wall before peering around the corner. He stands guard.

From here, Dusty can see the back of the vast room. There is no wall; it's wide open, revealing a view of the amber sun, dying on the horizon.

He looks up. The ceiling is hundreds of feet high, churning with the same dark clouds as the hallway. The back quarter of the ceiling is wide open, like the back of the room itself.

Dusty scoots forward, trying to peer under Scraggle's arm to see what's going on. He can see the giant insect guards filing up the hallway and layering into a half-circle, facing the center of the room.

The object of their gaze: a massive liquid-filled bubble, floating a few inches off the ground. The size of a giant whale, the oval bubble subtly and hypnotically changes shape, but remains tethered to the center of the room by a tube on its far end, reminiscent of a neck. This neck is nearly thirty feet thick, with a skin that is more milky and pale than the crystal clarity of the liquid bubble that it supports. The eel-like neck is clamped into place. A giant collar and heavy chains rooted to the temple floor hold it up, confining the liquid bubble to the center of the room. Below the collar, the neck snakes downward into a boundless pit. Down, down, into the planet's core, a molten-red glow emanates from the depths. Behind the neck are dark obsidian statues of bizarre creatures, lining the open edge of the back of the temple.

The amber sun is nearly gone, about to set over the horizon.

The last of the giant insect guards finishes filing into the half-circle.

The giant insect guard closest to the corner where Scraggle and Dusty hide turns around, breaking out of formation and marching directly towards them.

Dusty pulls backward, unsure of where to go. Scraggle looks back at him and raises his enormous hand, then lowers it, as if to say, "It's okay." But the giant insect guard continues marching straight towards them. There's nowhere to go, unless maybe Scraggle were to lift and carry him while they made a mad dash for the back of the room, down the giant pyramid steps. But Scraggle does not flinch.

At that moment, the guard stops directly around the corner from them and pulls a lever on the ground.

The crates lining the side of the hallway start to slowly move: it's a conveyer belt, moving the next animal in the line of cages toward the floating liquid bubble.

The giant insects start to chant.

Humming and eerie clicking fill the air with a phantom lullaby.

As the conveyer belt pulls a crate toward the floating liquid, Dusty can see the animal inside: it's a coyote. Pressed up against the back of the crate, its paws scraping at the bottom as it tries to back up, but there is nowhere to go. The crate enters the liquid bubble with ease, almost as if the bubble were aware; swallowing it.

The giant insect guard hits the lever again and the belt stops. Another giant insect guard in the center of the half-circle steps forward and carefully places his spear into the liquid, using the tip of the spear to unlock the crate, while carefully avoiding physical contact with the liquid himself. The coyote floats upward out of the crate, vulnerable, twitching with fear. A spectacular but graceful charge of electricity goes through the liquid bubble and down the neck.

Moments later, a flickering light fills the temple walls. Something is moving up through the neck — a glowing, translucent being, of a shimmering copper color with flickering hints of pale blue. The chanting stops.

All goes quiet....

Not a single click or shift of movement can be heard.

It is breathtaking. Its eyes are black, but its body is something ethereal, like an angel. It floats with a cloak-like skin around it that appears to be hiding a slender frame underneath. It must be about fifteen feet tall, with a head that seems to be made out of light, but hooded in the same flowing, translucent skin that cloaks the body. It has huge dark cavities instead of eyes, like the sunken sockets of a human skull, with never-ending depth; endless black holes. The way it moves is effortless and hypnotic, as if it's not moving at all, but instead everything else is moving towards it.

The world is in a trance.

The coyote which once squirmed with such frantic desire to escape has now become stunningly still, entranced as the angelic creature grows closer. As it approaches the coyote it slowly begins to open up its cloak-covered body, spreading apart, like giant wings. Blinding light shines from its insides. It spans open twenty feet, effortlessly, as if it could spread a hundred feet — a thousand — as far as it pleased.

The coyote is drawn in towards it, helplessly. The electricity of the liquid starts to build. The coyote looks aware again, as if it has awoken from a dream, but its body is still paralyzed, its eyes desperately searching, as it is pulled closer and closer, until it is finally engulfed. The angel closes its wing-like cloak around the coyote. The shape of the coyote can be seen beneath the cloak-like skin, as the angel embraces it tightly. The coyote's body stops moving;

it appears to be still and at peace, curled up like a baby in the womb.

Then suddenly, frantic electricity scatters throughout the liquid bubble. Lightning shoots out from the coyote's body, a warm, sanguine color seeping from it, as it struggles and twitches violently. The redness is absorbed into the angelic creature's body, turning it a deeper and deeper crimson. The lightning begins to take on a red hue as well, its frequency and power building exponentially to a crescendo, as it concentrates into one final deep crimson burst of light. It shines out the back of the temple and shoots across the horizon, illuminating the sky and beaming down the neck of the liquid into the center of the planet. Dusty has seen this burst of red before, the same as the one that occurred as Scraggle's family watched from their rooftop.

The giant insect guards bow before the blinding explosion of light, dropping their heads to the ground.

Scraggle is hunched and ready, as if he has been waiting for this moment. He turns back to Dusty, scooping him onto his back. With the giant insect guards still bowing before the liquid bubble, Scraggle makes a stealthy dash, carrying Dusty toward the back of the temple. Dusty looks back.

The angelic creature makes its first quick movement as it abruptly spreads open its wings, dropping the coyote's body. It then jolts backwards down the neck, disappearing into the underbelly of the planet, like a recoiling snake or a tongue darting back into a throat.

The coyote hits the temple floor, making a hard, rigid noise — stone on stone. The once-responsive and warm blood-pumping body is now cold black stone. Fur and flesh have turned to dark obsidian rock, frozen in the shape of its last moments.

Now, at the back of the temple, Scraggle slides behind the statue of a large, reptilian-looking creature just as the giant insects raise their heads from their bow.

A brooding, dark cloud then disperses out of the liquid, like smoke from an extinguished fire, and spreads through the roof of the temple, joining the dark kinetic clouds that cover the temple's ceiling.

As Scraggle begins to climb down the pyramid, Dusty can see the giant insects at the center of the half-circle grab long spears with large hooks on the end and sweep under the liquid bubble, hooking the coyote's stone figure. Together, they pull the new statue out from under the liquid sphere; again, they are careful not to touch the bubble.

Scraggle carries Dusty, dodging through a forest of obsidian. Every inch of the back of the pyramid is piled with what Dusty can now tell is a graveyard full of sacrificial statues, their last moments frozen in black stone. As they make their way down the giant steps through the assortment of statues, the amber sun begins to wearily reverse its decent, climbing the horizon.

At the bottom of the pyramid, Scraggle steps out of the clutter. When he turns, Dusty can see the obsidian graveyard stretching on and on, endlessly, into the shadows of a deep valley, and off into the horizon. *Annihilation — trophies of death, as far as the eye can see — cast in the permanent, dim glow of the amber sun.*

Dusty now realizes that Scraggle must have had the snake in his crate as collateral, knowing that the insect guards travel around demanding a sacrifice from each home — a sacrifice that they feed to the ghostly creature connected to the core of their planet, preventing their amber sun from disappearing over the horizon.

Scraggle cuts to the left, taking them out of the graveyard and onto a dirt path.

The path curves around. It's taking them toward the front of the temple. It looks deserted. Parked in front is the same train of carriages that the giant insect guards had put Dusty on after capturing him, but all the crates have been removed. The train sits on a well-worn and wide path, twisting down from the temple and oscillating through the hills speckled with faint blue lights emanating from the homes of the town below.

Another blood-red light bursts from the top of the temple above them, filling the sky. And the amber sun again creaks a few degrees higher on the horizon.

Scraggle lowers Dusty onto the first section of the train. This carriage has no crates — just a hollowed-out compartment, at the head of which six empty harnesses sit on the ground, belonging to whatever unknown beasts that had been pulling it.

Scraggle goes around to the back of the carriage. Dusty can hear a latching sound behind him. Then it's quiet…very quiet.

Dust struggles to flip around, trying to spot Scraggle, pulling himself to the edge of the hollow compartment. He peers over the side, looking in the direction where Scraggle went.

He's gone.

Dusty tries to stand up…he can feel his muscles feebly twitching, but they will not straighten.

He relents, collapsing back down.

The air feels crisp.

A tiny flickering entity floats in the air next to him. It spins around and pushes itself back up, dancing in the air, like a jellyfish. A galaxy of lights spark within its lucid body, shutting off and on, as Dusty imagines entire solar systems birthing and dying, eons of time drifting by in its minute frame.

Thump!

Steady drumming, thumps pound the ground.

It's coming from behind him. Dusty tilts his head back.

Scraggle approaches, guiding a large four-legged beast beside him. The beast is the size of a rhino; its solid frame knocks dust particles into the air as its thick legs thump upon the dirt path. It has a head like an aardvark, with a long snout and tiny mouth at the end, and long droopy ears. In the dim light, its wooly fur coat is a deep muddy brown.

With great haste and intense focus, Scraggle goes to work, wrapping one of the carriage's harnesses around the wooly beast and unhooking the other five, tossing them aside. He then jumps aboard and grabs the reins, jolting himself and Dusty backward as they start off down the path. Free from the burden of a long train, the carriage moves swiftly. The wooly beast strides with sudden astonishing grace, galloping with ease and familiarity as it guides them down into the hills.

The path takes them into the town. Dusty can see the homes up close. They are made of a woven and polished version of the hut material. Some are elaborate — multiple stories high — many of them with dome-shaped centers, the glow of blue lanterns spilling out of their small, but numerous windows.

The town's creatures are all outside by their homes, kneeling and bowing towards the temple. These inhabitants appear to be of a cream color, though it's hard to tell in the amber light. They are fuzzy creatures with flat heads and long snouts that nearly come to a point, like a tamandua, with equally fuzzy sloth-like arms and lower bodies, similar to that of a standing bear. They look up in disbelief as the carriage rides by.

The third burst of red light shines from the temple. Many of the towns-creatures are able to draw their attention back to the temple and bow before the light, but some are too shocked to unlock their gaze from the unruly carriage and its curious occupant.

Scraggle steers onward with unwavering focus. Dusty's head bounces against the side of the carriage as it bumps along the path. Watching him, the towns-creatures turn their heads, but never shift their bodies away from their source of worship: the amber sun, stuck on the horizon, refusing to rise any further, just as it did when Scraggle's family watched from the roof. There it hangs — never quite setting — never fully rising.

As they leave the town, the road becomes less-traveled and uneven, occasionally bouncing Dusty's body into the air for brief moments. They roll over empty hills and valleys, until they arrive at the location of Scraggle's hut.

But there is no hut.

In its place lies a pile of beaten down rubble. Demolished.

Nothing but debris.

Scraggle slows the carriage down, but does not stop. He continues past the remains of the hut and up the side of the hill. The path they had been following has now completely faded into the natural terrain. The carriage wobbles along the side of the hill and comes to a stop a hundred yards or so past the hut's remains.

Scraggle jumps down from the carriage. He desperately scrambles along the side of the hill, uncovering a small boulder hidden under the vegetation. Fresh dirt is scattered around the boulder and it looks as though it has recently been moved. When Scraggle moves it now, a small tunnel leading into the interior of the hillside is revealed.

Scraggle pokes his head inside the tunnel, searching frantically. A low, doleful moan escapes from deep within his chest.

A faint rumbling noise interrupts. Scraggle lifts his head back out of the hillside. Dusty can see the deep sorrow and longing cut across his brow as he alerts his attention back up the path from whence they'd just come. Dusty tilts his head back, following Scraggle's gaze.

In the distance, through the hills, storms a river of giant insect guards, marching along the path towards them.

Scraggle springs over to Dusty, lifting him out of the carriage, carrying him down the hill and through the valley, toward the edge of the dense jungle. Dusty recognizes the terrain from when he first entered this world.

At that moment, Dusty sees the tunnel that had brought him here. Scraggle looks back; the giant insect guards are still far off in the distance.

He carries Dusty into the tunnel, squeezing by the boulder that Dusty had previously managed to roll out of the way. Dusty thinks of the pleasant surprise he felt when he was able to budge the boulder. It had been a possibility that had come true, hoped and intended, but now the idea of such physical ability seems dully foreign, like an unattainable dream soaring away from him. He longs for a connection to his own body — his limbs, his torso, his fingers, his skin. Why should these things be called *his*, unless they care about *his* will?

Scraggle crawls through the dim tunnel swiftly, pulling Dusty behind him. This time, the dim light guiding them forward is no longer amber: it is a pale white, reminding Dusty of the moonlight when he left home.

Though Scraggle is trying to be careful, Dusty can tell that the urgency of their scramble forward is scraping and cutting into the back of his body and legs, his dead weight on the ground catching every spiny branch and jagged rock underneath the moss. But it does not bother him. Besides, he can barely feel it, and the disillusionment felt between him and his own body has become an unyielding, nearly hypnotic distraction from the thought of their pursuers.

Before he knows it, they have come to a stop. He tilts his head back. Scraggle is placing his hand against the moon engraving. The stone door slides down, revealing billions of stars, silently twinkling in the black void. Scraggle lifts Dusty, carrying him onto the stone slab sitting on the edge of space.

Scraggle walks to the center of the stone floor, gently placing Dusty down.

Scraggle crouches down beside him. Dusty wants to say something, but nothing comes out. He notices the soft texture of the fur and shiny black whiskers on Scraggle's long lion-like muzzle.

Scraggle places his hand across Dusty's chest and shoulder. Indeed, the hands that were once a source of dread and alarm have become a trigger for comfort. To Dusty, their shape is now keen, unique, and magical. Quite simply — *he likes them.*

Scraggle closes his matte-black eyes and bows his head for a moment...

...then opens them once more to look at Dusty...

...before he turns to leave.

Dusty watches him go. The stone door with the engraving of the moon on it slowly closes behind him. The ground begins to tremble and slowly move upward, gaining speed, traveling through space along the endless wall. Dusty sees the wall become blurry as the speed increases. Suddenly, the other three walls jut down around him. Up and up he flies, approaching a pale dim light above him, with seemingly infinite and effortless speed. At first, the dim light looks far away, like a faint star — and then suddenly very close. The ground rumbles to a stop beneath the light. It is in the center of the same pyramid ceiling that he first crawled into.

Except the color of the light, the room is eerily the same as when he had first entered it. *But he is not.* He looks down at his arm where he was bitten. In this light, the discoloration is a dark grayish-brown with a peculiar silver shimmer underneath it. The round stone door to the tunnel rumbles open.

Dusty turns onto his belly, crawling, fighting for energy. He inches out the door and into the dirt tunnel. His body continues to betray him, indifferent to his will. But oddly, once again, the bitten arm seems to be the only part of his body with any strength. He relies on it to pull himself forward, inch by inch. He slowly makes his way out of the dirt tunnel into the concrete tunnel, following the trickling water as it leads him into the larger tunnel connected to the arroyo. He can see the moonlight up ahead. He crawls through the hard rocks, using his last bit of will to pull himself out of the tunnel and into the night air.

He turns onto his back.

He can feel the sting in his joints and the dryness of his throat. He looks up at the moon, full and bright, and not far in the sky from when he left. He closes his eyes.

Chapter 8
JUICE, MILK, LEAVES

Dusty wakes up inside a dark room. Fluorescent light creeps in from under the door. He smells food— beside him, on a side table — a covered cafeteria tray. His instincts take over: he reaches for it.

He notices his left arm is connected to an IV, but this does not interrupt him. He uncovers the food and devours it, barely paying attention to what it is — some chicken tenders maybe, macaroni and cheese, potato salad, a roll, maybe some other stuff — something sweet? But either way, he's eaten it already. He is drinking the juice and milk almost simultaneously when suddenly, he stops.

Across from him, asleep in a chair, is his sister. She looks like a sketching. Her head rests on her soft canvas purse, atop a small round table. The light from under the door paints long shadows across her features and onto the wall.

The room is still. Cold and sterile.

His arm itches; he looks down. He is clothed in a sea-green hospital gown.

He takes the IV out of his left arm. On his right arm, the discoloration from the bite has spread all the way up to his shoulder.

He pulls down the neck of his hospital gown; the grayish-brown color has spread to his chest and down onto his abdomen. And there is a small bandage on the right side of his torso.

He lifts the gown up to examine it. He takes the bandage off; underneath it is a small, perfectly circular hole about the circumference of a pencil and an eighth inch deep cut out of his skin.

The wound looks fresh, precise, and surgical — a sample of the discolored skin taken from his body. He brushes over it with his fingers. Blood begins to rise up; he puts the bandage back on.

Suddenly, he remembers the hip he landed on when the giant insect guards dropped him into the cage; he squints and rubs his hand over it...it seems fine... perfectly fine. But his legs are still under the sheets.

He pulls the sheets aside. His legs appear unharmed: no breaks, no bruises, no scrapes, or scars — utterly unharmed. He tries to move them — they respond — they're moving — they're his again, but — but he is unsure of what to tell them.

He slowly slips to the edge of the bed and slides his legs off the side. He stands up, feeling the icy linoleum as it sticks to his warm feet. His wobbly limbs absorb the solid ground, sending shocks all the way up his body. Still holding on, he walks along the side of the bed.

He begins to remember what made his legs his own; it was that he never had to tell them anything. They knew. They knew as well as he did. He lets go of the bed. Finding new strength with each small step, he walks to the door.

He looks out the small rectangular window into the hallway.

It's empty.

He turns back and looks around the room. At the foot of the bed, he finds a pen and clipboard.

He looks over at his sister, etched into the shadows, like a life-size painting, her silhouette carved across the room.

He rips a little piece of paper from the clipboard and holds the pen up ready to write… nothing comes out.

He puts the clipboard back and turns to the door, silently sneaking out into the hallway.

The hospital looks empty, but he can hear voices up ahead.

He follows the exit sign, ducking into a stairwell.

Hollow, metal creaks echo as the door closes behind him. He tries to swiftly glide down the stairs, but — still getting used to his limbs — he bounces off the railings and stumbles into the wall, sending loud industrial vibrations howling up and down the stairwell.

Gaining control of himself, he pauses in silence, waiting, listening for a door to open and someone to look in…but there are only the lonely creaks from the modular steel…settling.

He tiptoes the rest of the way down to the bottom floor. He inches the door open just enough to peer out.

Across the hall, a tall reception desk wall encloses an office area that runs the length of the hallway. Down on the right, at the corner where the hallway meets another perpendicular hallway, there appears to be someone sitting at a reception desk. Past the perpendicular hallway are two layers of automatic sliding glass doors. Two figures dressed in long, white jackets are walking out the doors, exiting into the night air.

Dusty inches the stairwell door open a little further until he can peek around it into the left side of the hallway — it's not as well lit, but it appears to be empty.

He crawls out into the hallway, helping the door slowly "click" closed behind him. He crawls across the hall, sliding up against the half-wall of the reception desk. Staying low, he begins to slink toward the exit.

He can hear the person shuffling in their chair and making sipping noises on the other side of the desk.

From the perpendicular hallway, he hears voices —

Footsteps coming closer.

He huddles even lower, crunching into a tight ball against the desk.

"Night, Geraldine."

Above him to the left, the receptionist responds. "Good night."

"See you later."

"Later."

Two pairs of feet pop into Dusty's view. They are heading away from him, exiting toward the automatic doors. The shoes are white and clean, but look anciently old. How could something so ridden with time look so sterile?

The doors open, and the back of their heads come into view — a man with long, black hair pulled into a ponytail and an abnormally short woman with auburn hair, both dressed in light blue hospital scrubs. They walk out into the nearly barren parking lot. After a few moments, the doors slowly close behind them.

It's quiet again.

Dusty moves closer to the perpendicular hallway.

A deep sigh from above him — and then talking again.

"If you only knew...what the hell...now and later..."

The receptionist's voice is aimed in Dusty's direction. Is she talking to someone behind him!? He turns around.

Nothing — just the dimly lit empty hallway from which he came.

She continues: "...now and later...I see you again, I see you again...it's a circle...which one were you...which one was..." She trails off in a mumble. She must be talking to herself.

Dusty turns back toward the automatic doors, inching forward and peering down the perpendicular hallway, then around the edge of the desk in the other direction.

Another nurse is coming.

Dusty jolts back against the desk.

Footsteps...

"Geraldine! Why am I still here? I've gotta... ugh! Just gotta get some sleep! Ha! You probably just woke up though."

"No. I really just don't sleep much — at all."

"Yeah, who does...? *Huuummmff.*" The nurse lets out a frustrated groan that turns musical. In a bluesy tone, she sings the words, "See you tomorrow!" as she steps through the automatic doors.

The doors linger open behind her.

The receptionist grumbles a response.

Dusty darts toward the doors, crouched low to the ground, quickly tiptoeing after the nurse, trying to keep enough distance so that she doesn't sense him there.

Through the first automatic door.

Staying low.

Is the receptionist looking?

He doesn't look back.

Out the second set of automatic doors.

Outside.

The nurse veers off to the right toward the parking lot, walking by a police cruiser parked by the front curb.

Dusty instantly ducks to the left, moving along the side of the building, hidden by the landscaping — decorative bushes and trees on his right and towering brown stucco on his left. He continues along the outer hospital wall.

Through the trees, he can see the nurse's car lights turn on. She drives out of the parking lot, turning towards the few lit buildings in the plaza at the center of town.

When he has reached the edge of the building, he walks through the end of the immense, desolate parking lot and into the empty streets, heading in the opposite direction of the plaza.

He walks in the middle of the road, the cool pavement under his bare feet.

The only light is an occasional modest street lamp, flickering murky yellow onto the curb. No people, no cars, no lights on inside the adobe homes.

Gusts of wind scrape dry leaves across the street, lifting them up into the air and tossing them back onto the side of the street where they began. His hospital gown and hair whip from side to side, twisting around him.

He walks by St. John's College and the small piñon covered hills behind it. The road begins to curve down to the left; he can now see the larger mountains. *He is close.*

He reaches his house, going past his bedroom window and down into the arroyo. He stops at the entrance to the tunnel.

There is no amber glow coming from inside, no pale moonlight shining in. He can barely see, but he can hear the water dripping from the ceiling. He goes in.

He feels his way through the dark; pebbles and sharp twigs bite into the nerves of his bare feet. The new feeling in his legs is perhaps even more acute and capable than ever before.

The air feels damp and cold, as if the sun from the day never came out to bake off any of the moisture.

He reaches the metal water hatch; it is still open in the same position as when he crawled out of it with one hand, and the same as when he first followed Scraggle and the amber glow inside. He crawls in.

Darkness becomes pitch blackness. Were it not for the cold damp concrete, he might as well be floating in space. He shuffles onward. He does not need light; the memory in his head is distinct. It leads him into the fresh dirt tunnel.

Crawling his way down to the stone engraved door, he cannot see a solitary thing, but he can feel the etching of the foreign planet on the stone door. He feels all around it, trying to mimic what he did before. *Nothing.* The stone feels solid and does not have the same crumbling sand texture as before. Knowing that it slides downward when it opens, he grips his fingers along the top edge of the door and pulls down on it. *Nothing.*

He tries to think. He can't. In a convulsion of frustration, he slams his shoulder against the door.

It remains the same.

He lies there, feeling the dull ache in his shoulder and the suffocating snugness of the earth around him, squeezing him as he tries to catch his breath.

The air is getting thinner.

He knows he can't turn around; it is too narrow. He tries digging his toes into the ground, lifting his torso while pushing himself backwards with his hands. He gains a few inches. Dirt piles up around his face, getting into his nose and ears. He tries to ignore it, inching, one tiny movement at a time. He shuffles backward, gaining a few more inches.

His shins and arms burn with lactic acid, but the panicked thought of suffocating in here won't let his arms release. He reaches with his toes again and again. Falling dirt forces his eyes to tear and squeeze shut. His arms tremble, but the bitten one seems to surge with adrenaline and refuses to let him slide back down, scraping for new ground and pushing, pushing. Suddenly, his toe feels concrete. He wriggles the rest of the way out, catching his breath and wiping the dirt from his eyes.

He crawls all the way back out of the tunnel and into the arroyo. He walks over to the spot where he had seen Scraggle standing, like an apparition in the moonlight.

He looks up at the sky.

He cannot see the moon, only clouds.

He knocks some of the dirt out of his hair and ears.

He sits.

He sits, until for a moment, he forgets himself and where he is.

He stands and walks back up the streets toward the hospital.

He walks into the hospital. When the receptionist sees him, she stands up, her eyes and mouth wide open, like a fish on ice.

Chapter 9
LINOLEUM

A nurse leads Dusty into his hospital room, keeping one hand on his shoulder, never taking her eyes off him. She keeps hold even as she closes the door behind them, as if he will evaporate into thin air if he is not seen and touched.

His sister is still there sleeping, the light from the hallway still casting her in long, elegant shadows. She looks permanently still, untouchable, eternal.

The nurse shuts the door hard, perhaps because she is agitated or perhaps to purposely awaken his picturesque sister to a more alarming reality. If it was for the latter, it works. The slumbering sketch lifts her head.

The nurse speaks with a gruff voice, anxiously pushing at his sister when she talks. "Hello!"

His sister is still climbing her way out of her dreams. When she sees Dusty, her eyes light up; she rushes toward him, embracing him tightly.

Her voice cracks. "Oh my God. You're awake…."

An effortless smile beams across her face.

The nurse retorts, "He was outside. And I don't mean outside the room. Not in the hallway. He was OUTSIDE — outside of the building!"

"What?"

"Outside of the hospital."

"He was outside? Well…just now?"

"Outside — just now. He was outside of the building here. He walked in…'strolled' in. That's why he's covered in dirt — just strolled back in, whistling Dixie…"

Most of his sister's smile remains, but her eyes have turned to a familiar worry. He remembers her eyes were not always like that, but for a long time now it has been their common state — unsettled and heavy.

"You were outside? Why were you outside? Are you okay...? Why do you keep disappearing? Is he okay? Why was he outside?"

"We don't know — he's not speaking."

His sister cracks a crooked smile. "Well...."

Her worried gaze never leaves him. Her eyes feel overwhelmingly kind, as if her concern were a liquid pouring out of her eyes, drowning them both.

The nurse is about to speak, but before she can...

"I went for a walk."

The nurse pauses, waiting for him to say something more.

His sister looks at the nurse, who seems out of place. His sister's breathing slows and her voice shifts inward. She hugs Dusty tight again and talks to him with her chin on his shoulder. "A walk...oh...are you okay? I...why do you keep disappearing? How did you end up outside? What were you doing out there...? What's going on — have you been sleep walking...? I'm glad you're awake, though..."

Her eyes well up. She pulls back a little to look at his face. He avoids her gaze, looking down.

"You know you're loved, don't you?"

The nurse is blocking most of the light from the hallway, but the pale hospital floor reflects the parking lot lights from outside the window. How can it look so dirty and clean at the same time? Shiny and buffed — not a speck of dust on it, but old and worn looking underneath — as if the stains have been adopted into its very structural fiber?

His sister pulls him close again, putting his chin over her shoulder. "We didn't know if you were gonna wake up. You've been asleep for a long time, a few days now, Sleepyhead." She squeezes him.

He lifts his arms to return the embrace. As he does, he can feel her attention shift to his discolored right arm. She is fighting not to say anything, but she is about to lose the battle.

He speaks first. "I want to go home."

Chapter 10
BURGUNDY

Dusty is in bed. The morning sunlight is peeping through his window. He watches it dance on the edge of the window sill where he first saw Scraggle's hand. He can hear the murmur of his sister's voice coming from the living room.

All of a sudden, an abrupt, violent thirst comes over him, like an ambushing disease — burning dryness, overwhelming his entire body — his throat becomes too parched to swallow. His hands feel tight and sunken, as if the skin will pull inward, collapsing his bones; his eyes sting as he blinks, the lids scratching at his eyeballs. He is forced up out of bed, instinctively stumbling towards the bathroom.

As he opens his bedroom door, his sister's voice becomes clearly audible.

"Maybe it's a fungus or…. Well, I had spots on my back — Tinea Versicolor — if that's how you pronounce it; I probably…. No, I know, but something like that…something like a — like a fungus. Could it spread that quickly? I know and I'm not — "

He hobbles across the hall; each step feels as if it is pulling the last hint of conscious energy out of him, as if he will fade away. But the fiery pain in his dry, cracking body produces a will of its own and pushes him forward, until his trembling hand grabs onto the faucet knob, twisting. He tilts his head to drink, inhaling every drop. The water cannot come out fast enough.

"Well, can't they rush it through? If it's an emergency, do they have some sort of priority listing? On…uh…but…yes, I hope so, but by the time they come back from the lab…it's spreading…"

He continues to gulp; then, in a single instant, the thirst subsides. The water suddenly seems revolting; he can feel it filling his nose, ears, and brain. He coughs some of it up.

His head feels better. He looks at his hands; the ailing dryness is gone, the skin smooth and vital again, as if it had never happened.

With his left arm, he reaches out and shuts the bathroom door. He can still hear his sister's muffled voice coming through the bathroom wall. He stays huddled over the sink, studying his right hand, gripped onto the faucet knob. The hand looks a little bigger than he remembers. Its color is a deeper grayish-brown than yesterday — and tiny hairs, like a short coat of fur — have begun to sprout all over it.

The fur goes up his forearm, to his upper arm and shoulder. He reaches with his left hand to touch his clavicle; the fur is there, too. It feels strangely soft when he moves his hand downward, and coarse and rough when rubbing upward.

He continues feeling up the side of his neck. The fur is there, too. He stops. He turns his gaze up slightly, toward the bottom of the mirror. The mirror has never been his friend. It has always had its own opinions, and ruthlessly forced them upon him, placing images and perceptions in his mind, which were not his own as far as he was concerned, and he wanted nothing to do with it. So, a long time ago, he had made it a point to avoid its perceptions of him altogether.

But nonetheless, here he finds himself, letting his gaze wander up his arm through the mirror.

His sister blurts out, "...who knows how — it's fast! I don't know. I can't tell for sure, I don't want to make him nervous. Okay, well, please, please, as soon as you know. Thank you, thank you!" She hangs up.

Gazing up his arm to his shoulder, his arm looks more angular than he remembers. And the dark fur has a slight shine to it — a glossy coat. It continues up his shoulder, onto the side of his neck. He gets to his face; there is no fur, no discoloration. As least he thinks not, because he quickly aborts this interest in the mirror's opinions, leaving the restroom.

He goes back to his room and throws on some pants and his dark burgundy zip-up hoodie — the only piece of clothing that he can ever remember specifically picking out himself. His sister had given him a few bucks at the flea market. It was when they first came to Santa Fe. And as she shopped around, he had stayed at a single booth run by an old man with thick white hair that naturally seemed to grow only upwards, as did his eyebrows. And in this booth was the burgundy hoodie, with ragtag canvas patches sewn onto the elbows and a deep, brimmed hood.

———

In the kitchen, his sister has prepared an uncharacteristically simple breakfast: cheddar cheese melted on wheat toast. This was also something their mother used to make, but unlike the egg rolls, his sister had been a verbally harsh critic of the dish she's now serving.

Dusty's hands are covered by the sleeves of his hoodie. His sister keeps looking up at him. She can see his discolored skin peeking out from the collar of his undershirt.

He eats fast but steady, big bites. His sleeves are greasy from holding the cheesy bread.

He looks up at her and smiles. She can't help but smile back, but the worry quickly returns to her face. She lets out a sigh. "Are you...? Do you feel okay?"

He nods the question away. He keeps eating.

She stops eating. "Does it hurt at all? Does it feel uncomfortable?"

She subconsciously grabs her own arms as if she is taking on the same skin condition — hugging herself.

She waits for a response, coaxing with her anxious, but caring eyes.

"...No. It doesn't...hurt...."

"How did you end up out there?"

He looks like he is about to speak, but for a long time nothing comes out.

She tries again. "Do you remember?"

Dusty chews on his bottom lip. Still, no words come.

"I just want to know why this happened," she says.

He stuffs the last piece of toast in his mouth. Out the window, he can see the spot where he first saw Scraggle's long majestic handprint before the rain washed it away.

After a while, his sister takes the plates to the sink.

Dusty sits at the table alone.

———

Later that day at school, Dusty sits at his desk, still wearing his dark burgundy hoodie — the sleeves still pulled down over his hands, the hood carefully bunched up around the right side of his neck — trying to hide.

He runs his fingers over the surface of his desk. This is where his sketches used to be. Someone has cleaned it off. Nothing is left of it, not a trace. Only harsh brush marks (maybe from steel wool), signs of the intense effort that it took to eliminate. The coyote image must have been deeply tattooed into the synthetic wood, months and months of time on the same sketch — same eyes, hairs, and ears — sketched over and over itself.

Miss Gutierrez is walking through the aisles, passing out a worksheet. She gets to Dusty; her acute stare cuts into him.

"Nice to have you back."

Dusty looks up and gives a quick gesture of acknowledgement to temper her gaze.

Finally, she moves on, but he still feels eyes on him.

Off to his right, Gabe has turned in his desk and his entire body is now shifted towards Dusty, staring directly at his neck. Gabe's eyes are narrow and a look of disgust hangs on his brow; his nose is snarled and his lip, curled. He looks as though he is going to blurt something out.

Dusty pulls his hoodie up higher on his neck. As this happens, his hand slips out of its sleeve and for a brief second, his dark, angular fingers and hard, pointed nails — like claws — are revealed.

Gabe's eyes widen; the look of disgust melts away, replaced with alarm and confusion. He turns away from Dusty, facing forward in his desk, stuck in a wondering stupor.

———

Outside at lunchtime, Dusty sits in his tree. He barely remembers eating his lunch, but he knows he did. Before he even made it to the tree, he had scarfed it down — as soon as he walked out of the classroom.

He does not look out over the school grounds as he used to. He doesn't notice the texture of the bark or the feel of the wind. And though he can hear it, he pays no mind to the noise from the students. It all feels like white noise — dull, yet intense — like a feverish sun, buzzing in an endless desert. He gazes downward at nothing, stoic.

The school bell rings.

As the kids file into the classroom, they talk and bump into one another, shuffling inside. Dusty is in the back as usual, but no one is within five feet of him. There seems to be a conscious effort to stay away from him. No one will even look in his direction. Used to avoiding other people's gazes, he feels strangely free. With the others avoiding him, he is free to inspect wherever he likes, but the freedom is empty; there is nowhere he cares to look.

After school, Dusty walks straight through the Native American graveyard, past his secret lookout spot on the edge of the arroyo, and down through the arroyo to the tunnel. He crawls in, making his way back, deeper into the tunnel. It gets narrower and narrower, claustrophobic and hot — heat from the day baking like an oven through the ground.

He finally arrives back at the circular portal engraved with the strange moon, but there is still no glow, still no way through the stone engraved door, and no sign of anything that has come or gone.

As he did before, he pulls with his toes and pushes with his hands, scooting backward through the tight earth around him, inch by inch. This time, his body seems strangely adept, and responsive to the challenge. His arms move his body weight with ease, pushing backward, until he eventually has room to turn around.

He crawls back out of the tunnel. He sits in the arroyo, covered in dirt from head to toe. The dirt quickly loses what little moisture it had and cakes, crumbling into dust.

He sees an empty beer bottle next to him. It looks like it could be fifty years old, but he knows it's probably only been there a few weeks.

He hears squeals and laughter in the distance. He looks up at the trampoline house, off to the right.

He sees the kids' heads pop up and down over the piñon trees.

After a moment, he looks back down at the dusty beer bottle. He picks it up and taps it against a rock; it lets out a hollow cough, but remains solid. He stands up and drops it on the rock; it bounces off, chiming out, still unbroken. He picks it up and carries it up to the top of the arroyo with him.

Looking down into the arroyo, he imagines flinging it outward, sending it flipping wildly through the air, and careening to the bottom, shattering into a thousand pieces. But he doesn't throw it. He turns and puts it outside his window sill, on the spot where he first saw Scraggle's hand. He heads back inside.

He lies in bed, staring at the beer bottle outside his window.

———

As the days pass, Dusty spends his nights outside in the arroyo, sitting by the entrance to the tunnel, looking up at the moon.

The amber glow does not return.

———

One morning, Dusty and his sister sit at breakfast. The breakfast is elaborate, even for her — soft scrambled eggs with Brie and wild mushrooms, dusted with chives; broiled tomatoes with garlic olive oil; toasted sourdough, also with garlic olive oil; grapefruit, with honey and mint.

"You're not hungry...? You had quite an appetite for a while there. You had a healthy..." The energy drains from his sister's voice, her eyes close and her head lowers.

Dusty studies her hand, limply laid out on the table in the morning sunlight like a tree branch, etched with little textured cells of dry, paper-like skin, separated by fine lines — the sunlight highlighting every crevice, and inside each crevice, more cracks and fissures — until the entire hand seems like it is made only of the dark splitting spaces between.

She raises her head again, but her voice has lost its buoyancy. "...it's healthy, it's good...made me feel like I was a good cook.... You might get hungry later when you're at school..."

Still, neither one of them eats.

Unsure of what to say anymore, she simply observes.

There is a great weight in his breath.

A forced calm.

He stares through the table in front of him. He scratches his arm. He can feel her staring, digging with her eyes, examining his skin discoloration. How far has it spread? Can she see it on his neck? His face? He lowers his head further, until the brim of his long hood blocks her view.

She cannot take it.

She stands up, pulls herself around the table, and wraps herself around him. Her voice is wild, battling with itself in an effort to sound steady and resolute. "I'm so sorry. We're going to fix everything. You're gonna be back to yourself. We will find out how to fix this, okay. I promise. You're going to be okay."

Dusty does not move.

She squeezes tighter.

He does not respond.

His shoulders expand and fall with his slow, deep breath.

He speaks. "I don't want to fix it."

Everything inside of her drops. She tries to answer; only a squeak comes out. She holds on tighter still, digging her chin over his shoulder.

Chapter 11
DAY TWENTY-NINE

At school, Miss Gutierrez is walking down the aisles, passing out graded papers. Dusty now wears his burgundy hoodie all the time. He sits with his hood on and his head tilted down. She slows as she approaches him, placing his graded paper on the desk. His sleeved arm reaches up and slides the paper off, stuffing it directly into his backpack without looking at it.

She stops and takes in a deep breath before speaking.

"Dustin…»

The chatter of the room lowers to a murmur.

He does not look up or acknowledge her in any way.

A moment passes.

She moves on.

———

Later, in the school bathroom, Dusty stands at the urinal. Someone is washing their hands behind him. Dusty is done, but he does not turn around. He waits for the person to leave. Once they are gone he goes to the sink.

He turns on the water — looking down at his hands, as the cool water spills over them. Both hands are now fully covered in the deep grayish-brown and short fur, like the coat of a Doberman. He stretches out one hand. The bones are pronounced, with veins and stringy muscles popping out under the fur. All his fingernails are now short claws.

He bends down to the running water, tilting his head to the side, drinking with eager gulps until he is sated. He turns to leave, avoiding the mirror — but out of his peripheral vision he is slashed with an image of himself. He can see the discoloration has spread onto the lower part of his face.

Outside, he walks up the creaking metal ramp to the classroom. When he is almost at the door, he sees someone waving from across the schoolyard at the back door to the main building — *it's the trampoline girl.*

He goes to wave, but with his hand tucked inside his hoodie, it turns into a half-wave.

They both stay there, staring across the school grounds at one another.

He wants to walk towards her.

He can feel his clawed hand gripping into a ball under his sleeve.

The classroom door swings out.

Miss Gutierrez holds it open for him. He goes inside.

———

It's the end of the school day. Students file toward the exit. Dusty, last to rise, makes for the door. Miss Gutierrez sits at her desk, aggressively clicking her pen. Dusty is almost outside.

"Dustin!…"

He stops.

"Are you ok?"

He stares back, as if he doesn't understand the question, but then he nods. She looks down and starts to speak again. "If you…"

But he is already gone.

———

Dusty sits in his secret spot, the little cave hidden on the edge of the arroyo. He looks off to the left at his house. Through the window, he can see his sister on the telephone, pacing, always keeping one hand on the closest piece of furniture, removing it only to rub her tumid red eyes.

He looks back out over the arroyo. Heads pop in and out of view over the trees in front of the trampoline house. Something is different; there is a new head with the other three — another boy, about Nathan's age.

Dusty lies back against the dirt.

The sun is setting; the air is warm.

He can hear the trampoliners giggling and the wind whirring through the arroyo.

He sleeps.

He wakes up. It is nearly dark. As he sits up, a startled jackrabbit scurries off from beside him. He looks over at his house. He doesn't see his sister anymore. He can hear the wind flapping through the arroyo more assertively now, but the laughter from the trampoliners has ceased. The only sound is a lonely metronomic creak. In between creaks, he sees the trampoline girl's head pop up over the trees; she is alone.

He crosses down into the arroyo and softly makes his way up the other side, arriving at the piñon tree just outside of the trampoline girl's property. He stealthily climbs up and settles into the same branch he had hidden on once before, shrouded by the shade and pine needles.

He watches.

She stops jumping and sits.

It's getting darker. The gold-brown color begins to fade from her hair, but oddly he can still see every strand, lifting and settling on the side of her neck. In great detail, he can make out the soft, tiny hairs on her skin, perked up by the night air. After a while, he quietly starts to climb down.

"Why are you leaving?"

He freezes.

He peers around the tree at her.

She is still sitting on the trampoline, looking down at her hands. "You can stay…if you want to."

He stands there, as he always is now — with the sleeves of his hoodie wrapped over his hands, the long, brimmed hood up, shrouding his head.

She lifts her head, staring back at him.

Her eyes pull him forward, carrying him to the wire fence around the yard.

He reaches to climb over. His sleeve slips, revealing one of his creature-like hands.

He looks up at her reaction.

She sees it…

…but when her eyes come back to meet his, her expression has not changed. Her eyes are still drawing him in. He pulls himself over the fence, approaching the trampoline.

She lies down.

He climbs on and lies down next to her.

They look up at the gray cloud-covered sky.

She looks over at him. She sees the brown fur on his neck and cheek.

He does not move; he lets her look.

After a while, she looks back up at the sky. She reaches out and holds his hand.

He turns to her; her mouth is curled into a slight grin. Her features are soft and sharp at the same time. A fervor in her crisp eyes, a sudden burst of white light floods into them, reflecting the moon as it reveals itself from behind the clouds.

Dusty looks up; the moon is full, suddenly illuminating the terrain, revealing hidden depths.

The air shifts.

Dusty feels light; a surge of effortless energy feeds into him.

His senses widen.

There is a presence nearby. He lifts his head.

The trampoline girl raises her head to see what he is looking at.

The Nathan boy stands near the house, bearing an unwelcoming glare. She gets off the trampoline, looking back for Dusty.

He's gone.

Alone, he wanders through the arroyo.

He stops.

Up ahead, he sees a familiar light: *the amber glow has returned to the tunnel.*

He scurries inside.

———

Dusty's sister begins to flip through a grayish-blue folder in front of her, labeled "DUSTIN

HALVEM". Miss Gutierrez is sitting back in her oversized chair, which dwarfs her stature, closely studying and mimicking Dusty's sister. It is as if she is trying to *become* her, emotionally — her gaze pushing, unconsciously coaxing, a response of dark concern from Dusty's sister.

The folder contains photocopies of Dusty's homework assignments — all of them — math problems, grammar worksheets, history questions; every assignment is unanswered. Instead, each page has a sketching of a strange creature with dark angular features, a long lion-like snout, and matte black eyes.

SCRAGGLE

Chapter 12
STONE

Dusty pushes against the large stone boulder. It takes far less effort for him to move, easily sliding out and slumping to the side. Before he is even out of the mossy tunnel, he hears the guttural moan, bellowing across the land and vibrating through the ground. His stomach turns and the taste of salt rises in his mouth…he tries to ignore it, stepping out into the amber world.

He takes in his surroundings; it looks the same as when he left. To his right is the impossibly dark and dense jungle, reaching forever upward into the fog ceiling. On his left, is the valley, swooping up into the hills.

He spots the ruins of Scraggle's hut on the nearby hillside.

The vines begin to wrap around him. He quickly brushes them off, hurrying into the valley.

The amber sun is about to disappear over the horizon.

Another guttural moan trembles throughout the land.

He approaches another boulder on the side of the hill, by the remains of the hut. He remembers this is where Scraggle had stopped and frantically searched while helping him escape, but now the boulder has been moved back into place, covering up the entrance into the hillside.

He walks on, approaching the ruins of the hut. He searches around...nothing but debris. The vines have wrapped themselves around most of the splintered wood and household trinkets. He pulls some of the vines off one of the larger pieces of debris — it's what's left of the bed where he lay while Scraggle's family cared for him.

He continues searching around. Only one object from the ruins is not covered in vines — the large stone cauldron. He walks over to it. Underneath it, he can see that there is a stack of burnt vegetation. In the air lingers the bitter, sandy smell of the stew. He touches the bottom. It's warm.

Suddenly, the blood red glow shoots across the sky from the mountain. He stands and looks up at the temple, watching as the deep red slowly disperses, rolling like a wave evaporating into dry sand. Now knowing what it means, he wonders what has been sacrificed, but his thoughts are interrupted by his senses.

He can feel something watching him.

He turns around, and as he does, something runs up and grabs his leg.

It's the Baby creature.

She holds on tight, rubbing her face against his knee like a purring cat. Dusty doesn't know why, but his instincts now tell him the Baby creature is a she. He can see the Aye-aye cat stepping out of the cave on the side of the hill where Scraggle had searched before. She calls out a muffled lullaby in her soft, well-traveling tone. The Baby creature responds, trying to go back toward her mother, while pulling Dusty's leg along with her.

He follows.

As he approaches, he notices there is something different about the Aye-aye cat. The once natural pride of her feline-like figure hangs heavy and defeated; the spirit that once coruscated from her wondrous, huge eyes looks as though it has been trampled and gutted out of her.

He stops a few yards in front of her.

The Baby creature keeps pulling.

He doesn't budge.

They stand there for a while.

Another pulse of red bloodies the sky. The Aye-aye cat hangs her head.

Dusty turns back and looks up at the temple. The amber sun, responding to the sacrifice, rises ever so slightly on the horizon.

———

Alone, Dusty hikes his way up the worn path toward the temple. The amber sun is now as high as it will budge, fifteen degrees above the horizon.

As Dusty approaches the town, he can see the tamandua-like creatures in their elaborate dwellings, blue lanterns flickering inside, casting their silhouettes across the windows. They make slurping noises, dipping their snouts into deep gourd-like bowls, while they speak simultaneously, overlapping one another with short, chattery whimpers and whines.

One catches sight of him, dropping its bowl and locking its gaze upon him, alerting its companions with frantic gestures.

Dusty treks on.

Before long, a crowd of towns-creatures has started to form behind him, keeping their curiosity and their distance, and steadily growing in number. Dusty can hear them, softly whimpering back and forth between one another. He does not look back. He keeps stalking toward the temple.

As he walks, he touches the fur on his neck. It has grown up onto his ears and over onto his jaw. He brushes his lean fingers over his forehead and down his face. He can feel that he is now completely covered.

Just then, the ground begins to rumble, but there is no guttural moan. The crowd of towns-creatures stop following and begin to scatter, rushing back into their homes.

Dusty squints. The collection train is approaching. Up ahead, giant insect guards are leading the long train of carriages down the path from the temple to collect the sacrifices.

Dusty veers off to the left, cutting between the town's dwellings, making his way toward the outskirts and into the untraveled hills; he wades through a sea of the pale feather-like plants, forging his way up toward the temple through the obscure terrain.

He pauses, nearly at the top of the mountain, staring up at the massive pyramid, its impressive stature bathed in amber light.

He hikes on. As he gets closer, he can see the dark valley that sweeps down behind it, the endless obsidian graveyard, a sea of once living creatures frozen in stone, and — for his purposes — a back entrance into the temple.

Before entering, he looks back down over the town. Has something been following him? He spies two silhouettes in the distance: towns-creatures, one tall and unusually slender compared to the rest of its kind, and the other one, rotund and short, supporting its weight by periodically grabbing onto its companion's upper arm. They stop when they notice Dusty is watching them, keeping their distance.

Dusty turns back toward the temple, slipping into the glooming graveyard and climbing up the layers of the pyramid. He can feel the weight of the graveyard gnawing at him as he weaves through tails, horns, and limbs of obsidian stone. When he is nearly at the top, he looks back again.

The two towns-creatures are still following him, maintaining the same distance, again stopping when he does.

Dusty refocuses and pulls himself up the final steps of the temple, huddling behind the statues on the edge of the vast temple room.

He scans the chamber.

There are no giant insect guards, only the immense floating liquid bubble attached to the massive chained neck leading down through the hole into the center of the planet. The bubble is empty, hypnotically shifting in limbo.

He looks up.

The thin layer of midnight-colored clouds fester on the ceiling. Dusty carefully moves around the liquid bubble and heads for the crates, checking each one as he slowly moves down the giant hallway, spiraling down into the belly of the temple. *But no Scraggle yet.*

Some of the caged creatures make loud noises, barking and yelling, desperately searching for acknowledgment that they somehow still exist to the outside world. Others whimper and beg, but most have simply passed out. A few are familiar: a jackrabbit, a goat. *Still, no Scraggle.*

Suddenly, he sees a shadow approaching, heading up the hallway. The hard pickaxe sound — a giant insect guard!

Adrenaline surges through Dusty. He bolts the other way, back up toward the temple room, alarmed at his body's uncanny swiftness and command of agility.

Reaching the vast chamber, he retreats behind the floating liquid bubble, returning to the shadows among the obsidian statues on the edge of the temple's descending steps. He ducks behind one of the statues and peers around it — watching, waiting.

His senses are intensely keen and specific. The thwacking impacts from the giant insect guard's numerous legs send twitches through his hyper-alert reflexes. He can even hear the crackling sound coming from the swarm of antennae on its head, and with strange certainty, he can tell how far away the sounds are.

Furthermore, as the giant insect guard approaches, the loud screeching of some of the caged creatures does not hinder Dusty from hearing the delicate and fearful breathing of others. *But there is something else his senses are picking up — behind him.*

He turns back and there in the distance — climbing up the side of the temple — are the two towns-creatures. They are a good distance away, near the base of the pyramid. They cannot see him — they are too preoccupied, clumsily struggling to make their way up the giant steps, squeezing through the statues, pushing and pulling each other in a curious panic. It will be a while before they get to the top.

Dusty turns back to the room; the giant insect guard's shadow is creeping up the hallway wall. Caged creatures screeching, louder and louder, with a higher and higher pitch, stabbing at Dusty's eardrums. The shadow stops.

The howl of one particular creature rises into hysteria. Dusty remembers which creature was making that particular call; it was a pale-skinned, bird-like creature with a human-sized head and small hands on the end of its featherless wings.

The guard's shadow now protrudes its mantis-like arm outward with a vial in hand and sprinkles droplets of a mysterious substance. The creature's howling starts to fade and the shadow moves on, until Dusty sees the giant insect guard appear in the flesh. It stops again, taking its time as it methodically sprinkles its sedative potion over the next shrieking creature, going one by one.

Dusty can feel the icy coldness of the hard obsidian statue he is hiding behind; it presses into his forearm as he leans against it. He looks up at its impressive stature. It stands on two legs; thick limbs and scaly skin lead up to its wide crocodilian mouth. Dusty imagines what the magnificent beast must have once been like when animated with life. He wonders about its qualities — not only the ones that would seem obvious, like its powerful movement and gruff nature — but its nuances and oddities, its quirks, the things about it that it would share with another of its kind, and that perhaps made it feel — small and significant, at the same time.

Hearing the giant insect moving closer again, Dusty shifts his gaze back to the hallway, but as he does, something catches his eye —

— a hand —

— from the statue on the other side of the one he is leaning against…the long bony fingers like giant spider legs…but they are no longer leathery or dynamic.

He stands up — walks toward it.

He stops, face to face with Scraggle.

Stone.

The face does not look scared…it looks as Scraggle always did: strange, knowing and intensely calm, and to Dusty — kind.

Behind him, Dusty can hear the giant insect guard getting closer. It must have seen him walking into plain view, but Dusty does not hide. He does not turn around; he just stands there, staring at the cold stone that used to be his…friend.

The giant insect's harsh footsteps are now immediate.

Dusty can hear the twisting grip of the spear being readied in its hands.

Dusty finally turns to face it.

The giant insect is thrown off by the steady and preternatural timing of Dusty's turn, but it quickly shakes it off, raising its spear and lunging into him. But Dusty dodges out of way to the right with strange power and instinctive agility.

Now behind the giant insect guard, Dusty reaches up, grabbing the hooded antennae, and yanking down hard, throwing the giant insect's head toward the ground. The strange antennae writhe and wiggle from his grip.

The giant insect guard is in shock, grabbing its injured head and flailing, struggling to find its orientation. But without warning, the giant insect's long, lobster-like tail instinctively whips toward Dusty with lightning speed and thunderous force. Dusty's sharp reflexes react; he leaps into the air, but he is too late to fully escape. It clips his legs in midair and sweeps his feet out from under him.

Before Dusty can even hit the ground, the giant insect has recovered, finding its footing efficiently with its long body and many legs. It whips around, facing Dusty and lowering its spear, keeping Dusty on the ground. It makes controlled jabs at him as Dusty scoots backward along the floor, dodging the blade.

Dusty glances back; the giant insect guard is forcing him toward the giant liquid bubble.

Dusty tries to roll off to the side, but the giant insect whips its tail, curling it to block him, and reshuffling its legs, so that Dusty continues to be forced back toward the massive bubble. The spear jabs are coming closer and becoming harder to dodge. Dusty tries to focus, grabbing at the spear, but misses, slicing his hand. He knows the next stab will get him, if he doesn't move back.

He scrambles backward as far as he can manage, giving himself enough room to get to his feet, but his back is now inches away from the liquid bubble. His clothes and the fur on his neck stand up, as if the bubble has a magnetic force pulling him towards it. The giant insect has taken advantage of the half-second it took Dusty to get to his feet. It now has a clear shot at his chest: it jabs.

Dusty grabs ahold of the spear just as it punctures into him, barely penetrating into his sternum. Dusty tries to hold his ground, struggling to keep the spear from going deeper into his own chest, but the giant insect only pushes harder. The spear digs a little deeper. Dusty pushes back on it with everything he has. The giant insect matches his force, leaning forward. The spear tremors with tension.

Something has to give.

Suddenly, Dusty dives backward, pulling the spear with him into the liquid bubble. The giant insect guard tumbles forward, unable to control its momentum, falling into the bubble after him.

Dusty floats upward, pulling the spear out of his sternum. His blood, weightless, separates and molds into perfect spherical droplets.

For a brief moment, time slows.

The giant insect guard begins to become aware of what has just happened. It begins to flail around, whipping and twisting in an uncontrollable panic, its fear unhinged by its firsthand knowledge of the fate of those who enter the liquid bubble. Dusty tries to swim to the edge of it, but he can't. The bubble has no gravity. He can't create any force to move himself.

He is trapped.

Dusty looks around. In front of him, the giant insect guard continues to thrash about in abject terror, with a seemingly endless supply of energy.

Then above, Dusty sees the spear, floating. He reaches for it. It's on the edge of his fingertips.

He's got it.

He stabs it downward through the liquid bubble, chipping it into the stone temple floor, using it to leverage himself away from the giant insect, to the edge of the bubble. But the edge stops him, an invisible force pulling inward that will not let him leave.

He repositions the spear, again jamming it down through the bottom of the bubble, spiking it into the floor. He pulls with all of his might. If the spear can break out of the bubble, then so can he.

He starts to pull through. His head is out — his shoulders. He relaxes a little to catch his breath, and it pulls him back in, up to his neck.

Suddenly, a pale ethereal light begins to flicker on the temple walls. Dusty knows that from below, the translucent, angelic creature is floating its way up the neck of the liquid bubble towards them.

He regains his composure, spiking the spear hard into the floor once more, leveraging himself forward with all the power he can muster into a single moment.

Next thing he knows, he is diving onto the temple floor.

The spear falls on the floor next to him.

He stumbles to his feet; as he does, he notices the two towns-creatures, the one long and skinny, and the other short and plump, standing at the edge of the room. They finally made it up the temple steps.

They just stay there... watching him.

Dusty narrows his gaze on the amber sun behind them in the distance.

The towns-creatures turn their heads as the angelic creature enters the room, floating up out of the neck and into the liquid bubble.

Dusty's gaze remains on the fading sun.

All noises stop — all shrieks, all whimpers, all breaths are taken over by the loud hum of silence, as if the world is deep underwater. The frantic energy of the flailing giant insect sways to stillness, entranced into sheepish and dreadful awe. The angelic creature begins spreading its flowing, cloak-like wings as it approaches the giant insect.

Dusty looks over to the right side of the liquid bubble at the lifeless statue that was once Scraggle. He then looks directly at the angelic creature; its sunken eyes — empty black holes, pulling light inward and consuming it into nothingness. He picks up the spear off the temple floor and cocks it back. The angelic creature comes closer, engulfing its prey in its embrace. Dusty has its glowing translucent head in his sights.

Suddenly, he is pulled off balance. The two towns-creatures have made their way over to him and are pulling his spear-wielding arm down and begging him to stop. The short one points to the sun and falls to its knees, pleading.

Dusty lowers his spear, letting his arm fall by his side. The tall creature still holds on to him, collapsing to its knees, exhausted, in prayer.

In the liquid bubble, the red glow begins to spread, seeping out from the giant insect's body. Dusty looks deep into the angelic creature's eyes as it sucks the life from its prey. The eyes are hollow and indifferent.

It's beautiful.

Immense with power and emptiness.

Dusty feels as if he is careening endlessly through space.

A particle of light, being swallowed into a black hole.

In a sudden flash, Dusty raises the spear, thrusting it into the liquid bubble and through the angel's glowing head.

The two towns-creatures shriek with horror, dropping their heads to the ground in disbelief.

As if a light switch has been turned off, the bright heavenly glow vanishes from the angelic creature's body. The spear still in its head, it collapses downward. It hits the bottom of the liquid bubble. The bubble bursts, sending the immense body of liquid pouring to the ground and outward, sliding Dusty and the two towns-creatures against the temple walls.

With no bubble to hold it up, the giant neck slides through its collar, falling back down into the molten depths of the planet.

As the liquid dissipates, the room is quiet again, except for the whimper of the two towns-creatures in the corner. Dusty rises to his feet. In the center of the room, he can see the angelic creature's pale, lifeless, jelly-like carcass. The giant mass of its prey — the giant insect guard — still fused into the embrace of its cloak-like wings, the spear sticking up, out of its translucent head.

Dusty stands there, feeling the liquid seep down his fur and off his fingertips, watching the amber sun on the horizon and the cold obsidian statue of Scraggle in the foreground. The sun will not fully set for a while and most of the giant insect guards are still out on the road, looking for creatures to sacrifice to the liquid bubble.

The whimpering softens. The short towns-creature scrambles to its feet and tries to lift the tall, thin one, pleading, but he will not budge.

Eventually, the short one scrambles back the way it came, leaving the other behind.

Dusty walks over and takes the spear from the once angelic creature's head, and walks back toward the crates along the hallway.

In the hallway, Dusty pokes the spear into the latch on top of the first cage. It pops open.

He goes down the line unlocking cage after cage. Most of the creatures are too timid to move — some are sedated; the occasional one bolts off, running away in a panic.

He comes to a cage that contains a large toad-like creature standing on two legs. It has a kind face with a tuft of sandy-colored hair on its head. Its eyes look knowingly at Dusty as he opens its cage. When the cage opens, it bows its head towards Dusty in thanks.

Then following Dusty's lead, it takes out a small stone-carved knife that it seems to have concealed in its cage and tries to open the next cage down the line. He can't seem to get it open. Dusty watches while opening the cage in front of him.

When he is done, he hands the toad-like creature the spear. It opens the cage. It smiles at Dusty and offers the spear back. Dusty motions for him to keep it. The toad nods back and continues down the line, freeing the other creatures one by one.

Dusty turns back, heading back up to the main temple room, past the thin whimpering towns-creature and the carcass of the once-angelic creature, into the stone graveyard, and down the back of the temple.

At the bottom of the temple, he cuts out of the graveyard, heading for the off-road route from which he came. Off to his left, he can see the giant insect guards with their train of cages, rushing back along the worn path toward the front of the temple.

He makes his way back down the hills, staying on the outskirts of town. From a distance, he can see the towns-creatures gathering in the road, stunned and unsure of what has happened. Beneath the shock, a whisper of hysteria is brewing.

He makes his way back to the debris of Scraggle's old hut. As he approaches, the Aye-aye cat and the Baby creature come out from the interior of the hillside. The Baby creature tries rushing towards him again, but the Aye-aye cat holds her child back, a knowing and fearful look in her eyes.

The amber sun is dropping on the horizon.

Faint screams and distressed bellows echo down from the town above.

Dusty gathers debris from the hut into a pile.

The Aye-aye cat has not moved. She stands, holding her child close, her grip growing tighter — her eyes fixed upon the sun.

Dusty tries to start a fire over the debris, rubbing sticks together.

He is failing.

The sun is getting lower; part of it falls behind the horizon. The Aye-aye cat continues to stand, watching it, while holding her child, as if she stared hard enough, the sun would rise back up into the sky by sheer force of her will.

Dusty throws the stick away. Grabbing a rock, he tries hitting it against another rock, placing the feathery leaves next to it, hoping to catch a spark.

Nothing.

The sun is almost gone. Only a sliver remains.

The Aye-aye cat lets out a whimper.

Dusty stops and turns to watch.

The sun disappears.

Mayhem can be heard from the town above.

The Aye-aye cat turns and walks over towards the kettle. Dusty watches. She takes out a liquid from a pouch on her side and rubs it along the bottom half of the kettle. She then picks up a piece of debris and strikes it along the kettle where she rubbed. It starts a small blue flame along the bottom of the kettle and on the piece of debris. She brings the piece over to Dusty's pile, lighting it up.

They sit around the fire, the Baby creature curled up at her mother's feet, shivering. Sporadic screams can be heard from the hills above. The Aye-aye cat and Dusty stare at the blue flame in silence. She is nervous and her breath is fast.

The screams become less frequent.

Eventually they stop.

The Aye-aye cat sighs with defeated exhaustion. She leans over and lays down on her side, resting her head on her hand a few inches away from Dusty. His eyes shift over to her, then back to the fire.

Hours pass.

The fire is dying. The vines creep closer, crawling onto the Aye-aye cat's back as she lies on the ground, holding her baby. Her eyes are open, but she does not budge. She has given in. Dusty reaches over and knocks the vines away with his hand. They recoil, but then slowly inch toward her again.

Time.

Dusty gathers more debris for the fire. The Aye-aye cat still lies on the ground, curled up with the her baby. The Baby creature twitches as it sleeps.

Dusty can feel the Aye-aye cat watching him. He glances over; she does not look away. Her huge eyes are half-open, tired, terminally exhausted, and wet, like she has been crying. The vines have crept up her back again and are making their way over her side.

Dusty stops gathering debris and brings what little is left back over to the fire, piling it nearby. Sparingly, he places a few pieces on the withering flame. It starts to grow again. The vines back away from the light of the fire. Dusty reaches over and knocks what's left of them off the Aye-aye cat's back. He sits back down, leaning back against the hillside.

The Aye-aye cat continues to watch him. After a moment, she reaches out with her fingers and runs them along the brown-grey fur on his forearm. He looks at her. She closes her eyes. He reaches his hand out and caresses her head.

Time.

Dusty puts the last piece of debris onto the fire. His eyes are heavy. He leans back.

Time spins on…

Dusty is nearly asleep, his hand on the Aye-aye cat's head as she sleeps. He slips between consciousness and oblivion. His eyes flutter open for a moment. Sections of fog, away from the jungle, begin to dissipate, revealing the sky. There is a faint, dim light in the blackness above him — a pale bluish circle; he has seen it before, touched it....

...consciousness fades.

A tiny — no bigger than a cricket — wolf-like creature crawls up Dusty's shirt. He does not feel it. His head slides to the side, falling deeper asleep. The fire is dying down. The vines come closer.

The fire goes out.

The world is black.

Chapter 13
WATER

Dusty awakens to the sound of the Baby creature squealing. Warm yellows and reds saturate his eyelids. There is light. He opens his eyes and sits up.

The Aye-aye cat is standing up ahead. The Baby creature on her shoulders is squeaking and bouncing with joy, but the Aye-aye cat is perfectly still, staring up at the once-dense jungle opposite the hills. Rays of light crack through the ceiling of remaining fog and filter through the trees.

She lifts the Baby creature off her shoulders, placing her on the ground. The Baby creature runs over to Dusty, pulling him by the arm. He rises to his feet and follows the Baby creature over to her mom.

The Aye-aye cat's eyes are wide with amazement and wild confusion. They watch as the light continues to disperse the fog and permeate the jungle, breaking apart the tenebrous and festering grime with rays of light.

A ray shines onto Dusty's face. He raises his hand as a visor. The Aye-aye cat looks at him, confused; she pulls his hand down. He smiles and walks forward toward the forest, putting his hand back up to shield his eyes. He turns back and motions for them to follow. The Baby creature runs after him. The Aye-aye cat slowly follows, in a trance of awe. Her eyes watering from over-absorption, she raises her hand as a visor, too.

They walk into the forest. Everything has new color — rich turquoise and purples, shades of green and yellow. They come into a clearing. Crisp blue water pours down moss-covered rocks into a pond. Further up the pond, Dusty recognizes creatures released from the cages in the temple, drinking, exploring. Across the pond, he spots the large toad-like creature who helped release them all, its tuft of sandy-colored hair shining in the sunlight, as it leaps its way up the moss-covered rocks.

The Baby creature leans down and drinks from the pond. She looks back up at her mom, then to Dusty.

He gets down on his knees to drink. As he reaches into the water, he can see his reflection. He does not recognize his own face. He has a snout, a dark feline nose and whiskers. His ears are now perched up atop his head. A half-fossa, half-human looking creature. *Oddly, this reflection feels more like himself than any before.*

The Baby creature lifts water in her hands and brings it to her mom. Most of it leaks out, but the Aye-aye cat licks what is left from her daughter's hands. She finally smiles, but there is still a deep sadness imbued behind her eyes.

The Baby creature jumps up, pulling at Dusty and her mom, hurrying them away from the pond, and weaving them in and out of the exotic plants along the edge of the Jungle.

Then, Dusty abruptly stops, recognizing where he is. The Baby creature runs ahead. They've curved back toward the hills, which are now painted golden-brown, streaked with turquoise vines and spotted with the shimmering white of the giant dandelion tops. She pulls her mom along with her.

Dusty stands in front of the tunnel. His heart rate slows. He sits down next to the boulder, remembering the first time he climbed out of it. He thinks of when he could barely move his fingers, when Scraggle carried him through it, to save him from the giant insect guards. He looks down at his hands — they always look different.

In the distance, he can hear the Baby creature's playful squeal and the dreamy tone of her mother's voice.

After a moment, he stands.

He sees them up ahead on the side of the hill. The sun has continued to rise, sparking the tops of the hills and delicately leaking into the valleys between. He walks toward them. Once the Baby creature is assured he is coming, she turns and runs up past where her home used to be, hopping toward the sunlit top of the hill. The Aye-aye cat watches from below, waiting for him.

Chapter 14
SNOW

Winter.

A sparse dusting of snow lies over the terrain.

The trampoline girl lies on her trampoline, bundled in a warm puffy jacket, gloves, and a tightly pulled knit cap, looking up at the stars in the night sky. Resting behind a long, thin layer of cirrus clouds, a full moon watches over the land.

She sits up, sensing something coming from the tree on the edge of the arroyo.

She watches.

She stands, walking up to the fence. One of the large, level branches is shaking; some of the snow has been brushed off of it.

The wind whistles through the arroyo.

The tree shivers in the moonlight.

Chapter 15

Wispy snowflakes drift in the soft wind, disintegrating as they touch the earth.

Dusty's sister, bundled up in a scarf and wool coat over her pajamas, walks out her front gate and down the long dirt driveway sprinkled with pebbles and piñon needles. The driveway twists down, meeting up with the lonely dirt road that Dusty used to take to school.

At the corner is the mailbox. She grabs the mail: one letter and a grocery store flyer. She closes the mailbox.

As she turns back toward the driveway, she stops. There, standing on the dirt road watching her, is a coyote. Its piercing eyes look strangely friendly and familiar.

She stays there…

…the condensation from her breath hitting the bitter air, the snowflakes swaying around her. She can feel the bite as the cold permeates into her fingertips. She turns and walks back up the drive.

The coyote stays, watching.